The Sailor

John Hagen

Dedication

To Ileana, my wife

Acknowledgement

Thanks for the legal advice from Sam Berman and Jeffery Manishen. Thanks to Dr. Gary Dvorkin for advice on publishing and content. Most of all, thanks to my wife for advice on neurophysiology and support.

Contents

Prologue

Death would be a certainty within 24 hours. The survival at sea course that he recently completed estimated survival at 1% after the first day in the ocean. Although confused initially, his memory returned. He surmised he hit his head when he fell off the boat and briefly became unconscious. The memory of precisely what happened escaped him. The life vest auto-inflated, as expected when he became immersed in the boundless sea. This kept his head above the water, preventing him from drowning. Two hundred nautical miles separated him from the closest shore, and the gravity of the events slowly returned to him. The warm waters in the area known as the Bermuda Triangle would surely result in death within 24 hours. He glanced around at the water, looking for his boat. Endless blue water and waves in all directions accounted for the only images that reached his field of vision. The sun beat down on him relentlessly, with no clouds in the sky to temper the intensity. The warm easterly trade winds caused gentle 5-foot waves that would elevate him enough so that he visualized a glimpse of the horizon. Nothing but water and waves as far as the horizon. The hopelessness of his predicament occupied his thoughts.

One month earlier.

Chapter 1

"Dr. Young, can you come to operating room 15? Dr. Yacoby is having another one of his meltdowns." Nina, the nurse, delivered the message slightly breathlessly. She had just run down the hall to Dr. Young's administrative office, about one hundred meters from the main operating room. Interrupted, Dr. Young completed the review of the most recent results of gastric bypasses. This analysis showed how the hospital compared to similar-sized hospitals. A report to the medical advisory committee later that day would follow. The poor results needed to be delivered to the committee without making them seem as bad as they appeared. Dr. Jeremy Young, the chief of surgery at a large community hospital, oversaw the 120 surgeons there. Jeremy had to ensure top-quality care from his surgery department and handle difficult personalities. Dr. Julian Yacoby, an orthopedic surgeon, had lately become a thorn in his side. His frequent episodes of unacceptable behavior on the surgical floor and in the operating room dominated Jeremy's time.

Dr. Jeremy Young, at age 57, became chief of surgery. He ran ten kilometers three or four times a week and was about six feet tall and trim, keeping in top physical shape. Handsome, with angular features to his jaw and nose, many nurses described him as hot. With three adult children, his marriage to Iona kept him happy and content. Being new at the job as chief, he had already dealt with several surgeons and their inappropriate behavior. The hospital no longer tolerated disruptive behavior. The hospital chose Jeremy to become chief of surgery partly because of his assurance to modify this behavior culture from surgeons.

About 10 years earlier, an anesthesiologist at a nearby community hospital killed his former lover, a recovery room nurse. He then killed himself. The coroner's inquest determined the anesthesiologist displayed plenty of indications that he steered himself down in a self-destructive and dangerous direction. Jeremy had considered the anesthesiologist a close friend earlier in his life. They became roommates during medical school. He lost touch with him over the past 20 years. It came as a great surprise when these tragedies occurred. The anesthesiologist exhibited multiple disruptive behavior episodes on the surgical floor, and no one challenged him during these episodes. Because he worked as a respected anesthesiologist, everyone else paid the price for his unacceptable behavior. It was difficult to keep anesthesiologists because of the province-wide shortage. The inquest concluded that earlier action would have avoided the tragedy. Because of this incident, zero tolerance for unacceptable behavior became the expected practice among surgeons and other staff, including those who worked at Dr. Young's hospital.

Dr. Young donned his surgical attire and went to operating room 15. Upon entering the room, a somber mood emanated from the traumatized staff. Things had quieted down, and silence prevailed. Although the total hip operation continued, the procedure had almost finished. The palpable tension in the room originated from the verbal beating that the scrub nurse Valerie had taken earlier in the case. Dr. Young saw a stream of tears coming out from underneath her mask, and she looked defeated.

"Can someone relieve Valerie so I can speak with her in my office?" Dr. Young said to the circulating nurse.

"Dr. Yakoby, when the surgery finishes, please drop around to my office?"

Dr. Young waited until Valerie removed her surgical gown, and they headed out to his office together. Only after closing the door and sitting down did he ask, "What happened in there, Valerie?"

Valerie said, "It became obvious from the moment he walked in this morning that there would be a problem. He ranted and raved about the patient being late for the hospital and how this disrupted his entire day. He refused to do the 'Time out' required for his case. Before starting the surgery, the orthopedic resident did this. When Julian came back in after scrubbing, he lit into me, saying I had the wrong equipment and to rectify the situation immediately. The equipment was perfect. He always used it, but his bad mood made me anxious about what would happen next. When I passed him the scalpel to start the operation, he picked it up and threw it against the wall. It stuck into the plaster. He said I gave him a #15 blade when he wanted a #11 blade, and what made me do something so stupid? Dr. Young, this is what I always give him; it has never been a problem. I have noticed lately he has been exceedingly difficult. I do not think I can work with him again; I don't feel safe."

Dr. Young replied in a calming voice, "I am so sorry to hear this. We have zero tolerance for unacceptable behavior among our surgeons. I am going to speak with him after he has finished the case. After I speak with him, I will have another conversation with you. I hope we can resolve this without you going through your union, which would be exceedingly difficult for the hospital and Dr. Yacoby, but the next steps will be up to you. I will support you in whichever direction you wish to proceed."

"Thank you, Dr. Young," she said as she dried the tears.

After Valerie left, Dr. Young made a few notes about what Valerie told him. The third occurrence in about 2 months resulted in another meeting with Dr. Yacoby. Two other times involved outbursts on the surgical floor. The first incident happened when one of the nursing students failed to give the antibiotic at the correct time. A second outburst occurred with the nurse manager a few weeks later when she confronted him about his poor attitude. Both times, Dr. Young met with Dr. Yacoby. The first principle Dr.

Young mandated was to determine the underline cause of the problem. Drugs and alcohol often cause inappropriate behavior, making it necessary for Dr. Young to exclude this as a plausible reason. Dr. Young observed that surgeons under stress from home life issues could display unacceptable behavior. This stress resulted in directing their angst toward the nursing staff. Burned out from years of overwork and being underappreciated caused further problems among surgeons. Jeremy thought about how he would approach this situation when Dr. Yacoby appeared at his door.

Dr. Young asked, "Please come in and have a seat, Julian. Thank you for dropping by. Valerie seemed quite upset. What happened?"

"All I ask is for competence. Why am I always targeted to have the most incompetent nurses at this hospital? Why can't they just do what they should so I can have a normal operating day? What do I have to do to get excellent nurses? I am sick and tired of their unprofessionalism. As chief of surgery, I expect you to do your job and get me good competent nurses regularly so I do not have this struggle every time I do a case."

"Valerie said that you picked up a knife and threw it against the wall, and it stuck into the plaster."

"What do you expect when she gives me such shitty equipment? I asked for a #11 blade, and she gave me a #15 blade.

How can I work with that?"

Dr. Young tried a different angle. "Julian, I am worried about you. This is the third time we have met in the past two months. Throwing a knife is not normal behavior for a surgeon. I will have to close your operating room for the day so we can do a complete investigation. I will determine whether the problems occurred because of incorrect equipment, as you suggested, or something else. I would also like you to undergo a drug and alcohol test to prove you are drug-free. Valerie is refusing to work with you. She does not feel safe."

Dr. Yakoby's face turned bright red, and his pupils dilated as he retorted, "Fuck you, Jeremy. I am losing an entire day of income because you're shutting down my operating room. I am not doing a bullshit urine drug screen. You are going to hear from my lawyer!" He stormed out of the room and slammed the door.

Dr. Young placed an emergency conference call with the CEO of the hospital and the chief of staff. We wanted to apprise them of the situation and his plans to close the operating room while investigating the meltdown.

The chief of staff suggested, "Instead of presenting the gastric bypass results at the Medical Advisory meeting tonight, we should discuss what to do with Dr. Yacoby instead. Can you invite Dr. Yacoby to attend as well?" Dr. Young readily agreed.

Jeremy Young failed to locate Julian Yacoby to invite him to the medical advisory committee. He did not answer his cell phone. No one answered at his home. Dr. Yacoby disappeared.

Chapter 2

The gun blasted off from the committee boat for the 5-minute warning before the start of the sailing race. The wind blew a pleasant breeze of 10 knots coming from the west. Jeremy Young sailed on Lake Ontario for the past 20 years and loved the camaraderie of his crew and weekly club racing events. Six others crewed on his 51-foot sailboat, all experienced sailors. Experts in their positions, they sailed the boat as fast as possible. The navigator set the timer for 5 minutes so that, ideally, the boat would cross the start line exactly as the starting gun fired. The angst at the beginning of the race occurred because all the boats tried for the best position to get the undisturbed wind for the best start. Common wisdom dictated that the boat that gets the best start determined the boat that would win the race. The navigator said, "We will aim next to the committee boat to start the race. This will give us clear air and about a boat length advantage to the next mark." The other ten boats at the start used the same strategy.

One minute left before the start, Jeremy bellowed, "Prepare to come about," followed instantaneously by the command, "Tacking!". The boat turned 90 degrees and headed for the ideal position on the start line close to the committee boat. Speed gave the 51-foot sailboat the best chance for the perfect start position. The larger boat sailed faster than 90% of the smaller boats. This gave them a clear advantage in attaining the best position at the start. With the perfect angle and timing, the sailboat aimed right for the committee boat end. The absence of boats downwind gave Jeremy the right of way for any boats if they tried to sneak in between him and the committee boat.

Out of nowhere, a J35 sailboat attempted to squeeze in between Jeremy and the committee boat. "Clear out of the way!" yelled Jeremy at the skipper of the J35, "You have no rights, and there is no room to let you in!"

The J35 skipper ignored the warning. "There is plenty of room, and you must let us in."

"I am holding my course. You will not make it. I have the right of way," yelled Jeremy.

Everything seemed to happen quickly following that. The J35 skipper realized 3 seconds too late that he would not make it and would soon smash into Jeremy's boat if he did not alter course. When he tried to alter course, the momentum forced him into the stern of the committee boat with a loud crack. The forestay snapped with the collision, and the momentum caused the mast to crumble slowly into the water. Pandemonium ensued as the J35 sailboat stopped moving through the water. The damaged boat bobbed helplessly with the mast dragging in the water, held on only by the backstays and shrouds.

The committee boat blasted off two warning shots to delay the race. Jeremy spun the boat into the wind, took the sails down, and started the engine to assist the damaged J35 sailboat. When he got alongside, the J35 skipper said, "You asshole, look what you've done to my boat."

Ignoring the comments, Jeremy said, "Is everybody all right? Is anyone injured? I have a pair of wire cutters you can use to cut the shrouds and backstay so that the mast does not put a hole in your boat." The navigator ran into the main salon, pulled out the wire cutters, and passed them over to the J35 skipper. They quickly divided all the attachments of the mast, and the mast sunk into Lake Ontario in about one hundred feet of water. They started their engine and headed to the shore with no further problems.

Later that evening, at the clubhouse, the commodore of the race fleet announced there would be an investigation into the accident. The police would be involved. They would interview the skippers, the crew of both boats and any other boats that witnessed the accident. The committee boat members watched the incident unfold, and they would be key to understanding what happened. The race officer, Ron Higgins, who viewed the incident from the committee boat, told Jeremy, "You may have been the right of way sailboat. But in the rules of racing, it clearly states that you must do whatever is necessary to avoid a collision. You failed to do this, and I am holding you responsible." Jeremy experienced the unfamiliar sinking sensation as his life was becoming unraveled.

It had been a rough week for Jeremy. At the medical advisory committee meeting the evening before, Jeremy discussed Dr. Yacoby's behavior in the operating room. He discussed how it shook up the nursing staff. He outlined his concerns that this was not normal behavior and, as per the *disruptive physician behavior policy*. "Something else in his life must be causing him to behave in this irrational fashion," Jeremy said to the chiefs who sat around the boardroom table.

The chief of Psychiatry, Robert Planter, spoke first. "It is you being way too hard on Dr. Yacoby. Surgery is a tough profession, and he is under tremendous stress. He has been on staff for 5 years, and there were never any problems until this incident. You are acting heavy-handed by closing his operating room and not giving him the benefit of the doubt. I see this happening repeatedly among our staff, where the chief insists on the staff behaving with unrealistic expectations. I agree with Dr. Yacoby that you are acting outside your authority to shut down the operating room and deprive him of his income for the day."

The chiefs of medicine and pediatrics agreed with the Chief of Psychiatry. As the conversation bounced around the room, if any of the chiefs of other departments agreed with Jeremy, they did not voice their support. The others condemned Jeremy's actions.

That Dr. Yacoby contacted at least two chiefs before the meeting became obvious to Jeremy. After carefully listening to the comments, Jeremy replied, "I am deeply disturbed by what I am hearing here. We have an operating room where the surgeon picked up a scalpel and threw it against the wall, where it stuck in the plaster. He might have injured someone. We have an operating room where the nurses refuse to work with him because they are not working in a safe environment. This is inappropriate behavior, and I won't tolerate this in my operating room. I attempted contact with Dr. Yacoby and am worried about his safety. I firmly believe something is wrong with him."

The head of psychiatry answered, "Well, we believe there is an issue with you. You have exceeded your authority, and we cannot tolerate this in our hospital."

Jeremy realized that he had lost the argument and failed to convince the others to agree with his actions. He picked up his laptop and papers and walked out of the meeting. Continuing the conversation with this group of chiefs wasted everyone's time. He would meet with the hospital's CEO and chief of staff to discuss his concerns later in the week. In the meantime, his powers as chief allowed him to close any operating room where safety concerns prevailed while he investigated.

Chapter 3

Jeremy always tried to do the "right thing." Even when others might disagree, being unable to let things go that seemed unfair or blatantly wrong caused him to voice his opinion. This sometimes led to discomfort for those around him. Expressing these strong viewpoints to do the "right thing" developed during high school. In high school, he became friends with Benji Martins. Benji, a Black student, fell into the minority racial category at the school. They became friends because they both ran on the track and field team of the high school. Jeremy ran fast at the longer distances, 1000-meter and 5000-meter events, while Benji bolted like a rocket in the 100-meter sprint. They acted like coaches, encouraging and congratulating each other when they raced to win.

Richard Hamley, the captain and star quarterback of the football team, yelled to Jeremy across the green lawn. "Hey Jeremy, how's it going?"

Jeremy crossed the lawn to speak with Richard. "Not bad. I dominated a race this morning and finished first in the 1000-meter event. Benji finished first in the 100-meter event."

"Why don't you join the football team?" asked Richard. "We would use you as an end receiver. With your speed, we would take the pennant."

Jeremy laughed. "I have butter fingers. The football falls from my hands the moment it touches them. Even if my life depended on it, I would drop the ball. How about asking Benji? He has fingers like Velcro, and he is faster than me."

Richard stared at Jeremy and said, "I will never have a black player on my team. The coach knows this. I would quit before allowing this. They would not allow that to happen because I am the best quarterback star this school has ever seen."

Jeremy, at a loss for words, remained silent. He heard that racism prevailed in the school, and the teachers lectured on what racism meant. The teachers gave little instruction about what to do when it stared you in the face. Richard, the most popular student at school, caused the girls to swoon when he walked by and delivered his seductive smile to them. All the guys at school admired him. They frequently said how he became an example to follow, being such a great guy. Jeremy heard no one say a negative word about him. Jeremy, confused, watched him walk away and said nothing.

Laying in bed that night, sleep evaded Jeremy. Benji, his friend and his biggest fan of his running achievements became targeted by a racist, yet he said nothing. Jeremy kept living through the conversation with Richard. Allowing something as egregious as what Richard said to pass by saying nothing made Jeremy ashamed of his inactions. In his mind, Jeremy acknowledged that by remaining silent, he endorsed Richard's racist views. He recognized that this became the reason racism persists today. He remembered his history teacher reciting the quote. "The only thing necessary for the triumph of evil is for good men to do nothing."

Jeremy whispered into his pillow, "I am not even a good man. I said nothing."

Sleep continued to evade Jeremy that night. He would confront Richard before football practice. The track ran outside the football field, and the practices occurred simultaneously. All day, Jeremy thought about his conversation with Richard and the potential outcomes. Jeremy envisioned this ending badly but would avoid a physical confrontation at all costs.

"Richard, I would like to talk with you," said Jeremy when he saw him on the football field.

"You've decided to join the winning team?" asked Richard, laughing.

"I want to understand what you meant when you said you would never have a black on the football team?" asked Jeremy.

The silence of Richard lasted for several seconds before he spoke. "So, you are one of those?"

Richard turned to the football field and yelled to his teammates, "Guys, get over here! We have one of those in our midst.

We need to teach him a lesson."

Ten of the biggest boys in the school came over to where Richard and Jeremy stood. They positioned themselves around Jeremy in a circle and started pushing him toward each other. Each time, they delivered a punch or kicked as Jeremy stumbled past. The group of boys started pushing Jeremy faster and faster, and the impact of the punches and kicks became more intense. The punishment would have continued, but the football team's coach appeared. The group of boys ran out onto the football field.

"Say one word of this to anyone, and we will do it again. We will make you watch while we do this to Benji," said Richard as he left to join his teammates.

Jeremy painfully went to the track and field clubhouse to wash up. His nose dripped with blood. His bruised body made it difficult for him to walk. Benji, the first person to see him, asked with authentic concern, "What happened to you?"

Jeremy told him about the events leading up to the beating. "And yesterday, Benji, I said nothing. I just stood there. I am so ashamed."

Benji hugged Jeremy and said, "Let it go, Jeremy. The world is full of terrible people. You live in a fantasy world. We are best friends, but you do not know what it is like being black and listening to this daily. Let it go."

"I can't, Benji," said Jeremy. Benji looked at Jeremy and understood the futility of talking sense into him. Benji also understood systemic racism as one of those unchanging realities of life that Jeremy must learn to accept. Nothing but hardship would come if Jeremy traveled down the path of righteousness. The facts remained simple. He was black, and Jeremy was white.

Two days later, Jeremy met with the coach and the school principal. While sitting around a small table in the office, Jeremy outlined the events of the encounter, including getting punched and kicked in the circle.

The coach responded first. "I am sorry that the team did that to you. I will speak with them and ensure this does not happen again. If it happens again, or they threaten you, come to me immediately. We have the best football team in the city and are going places. It would be a shame if something like this derailed us after all the effort we have put into the rebuilding."

"I am not concerned so much about what happened to me. I will be a little more careful next time and prevent those bullies from cornering me again," Jeremy said. "But why is it that 10% of the students at this school are African American? Yet there are no African American teachers and no African American players on the football team."

The principal answered angrily. "I am not sure I like where

this conversation is going. We offer them jobs as teachers; they just do not stick around. No black kids even tried out for the team this year, so do not imply that anything we do is improper."

"Why would a black teacher or student want to be around when they are unwelcome?" asked Jeremy.

The principal and the coach glared at Jeremy in silence. Challenged by a student who implied they allowed a racist environment angered them. It momentarily caused them to remain speechless. The school functioned well, with top grades and other academic achievements at all levels. Many of the elite athletes on the team expected football scholarship offerings to the best universities for the fall. This winning football team performed so well this season. The principal and the coach proudly boasted of their accomplishments to anyone who would listen.

Then the principal smiled at Jeremy and said, "Well, son, I'll look into it and see what I can do." The conversation finished with that hollow promise.

As Jeremy walked away from the office, he developed a tingling sensation in the back of his neck for the first time. This discussion with the principal and coach yielded no results. Jeremy constructed his plan to wait for a month and then have another dialogue with the principal. Multiple attempts failed to arrange another meeting with the principal a month later. The unanswered phone calls and messages denied any hope of this occurring.

Jeremy thought long and hard about his next step. He wrote a carefully constructed letter to the Human Rights Board. The research by Jeremy showed systemic racism ran throughout the school. He knew changing direction would be exceedingly difficult, if not impossible. In his letter, he outlined the details of his experience with racism. When he discussed the meeting with the principal and coach, he described their dismissive attitude. They shifted the blame from the organizational practices onto the Black teachers and students. Jeremy eloquently wrote that a culture change required guidance from experts such as them. The highest level of the school structure needed education on anti-black racism. Two weeks later, the response from the Human Rights Board, renowned for its red tape and slowness, surpassed Jeremy's expectations.

The explosive effect shook the school to its core. Interrupting the English literature class, the teacher escorted Jeremy to meet with the principal. The principal's fury emanated from his every pore. He paced around his office, and his face became bright red. The veins in his neck bulged, and his anger seethed throughout his body, causing the pupils to dilate. Jeremy witnessed no one so upset in his 17 years of life. Jeremy listened to the principal's tirade about the tribunal's investigation. The yelling lasted for 15 minutes, with frequent finger-pointing at Jeremy. Improper and unfair accusations flew at Jeremy from the raging principal. Jeremy sat there, fascinated with the reaction, thinking as he watched the histrionics that this defied normal behavior. Once the inquiry findings become public, the principal will face serious repercussions and will have to justify himself. Finally, after an exhaustive rage, the principal dismissed Jeremy from the office.

When the tribunal results became public, the school board fired the coach and the principal. They dissembled the football team for a year to incorporate anti-black racism prevention into their culture. The recommendations incorporated anti-black racism policies and procedures throughout the city school board system. This made national news. Jeremy had done the "right thing."

Chapter 4

Jeremy Young made his usual rounds on the surgical floor the following morning. He performed gastric bypasses on four patients the day before. He made rounds to ensure that the discharge from the hospital proceeded uneventfully. The first three patients dressed and packed their things in their bags to leave the hospital by 7 AM. Their husbands confirmed to be on their way to pick them up. The uneventful surgery and postoperative course resulted in minor discomfort. They expected Jeremy Young to help them lose 100 pounds after the successful surgery. With the usual postoperative instructions and a follow-up organized the following day in the bariatric clinic, they prepared to leave.

Dr. Young entered the room of the fourth patient, Mrs. Charlene Simpson, and said, "How are you today, Mrs. Simpson? The surgery proceeded well yesterday, and no complications or problems occurred."

Mrs. Simpson said, "Although I am fine and have only minor discomfort, I have three young kids at home. I'm wondering if I might stay in the hospital another day to get some rest."

"The usual expectation is to go home on the first postoperative day unless there are some medical-related concerns. If you are not in too much discomfort, let's see how you are by later in the afternoon, and if you're fine, perhaps you can go home then. Would that be OK?"

"I suppose," she said.

"I will ask our discharge planner to come by to see you and see if there's anything we can do to help you at home to make things easier for you." Dr. Young replied. "If we can help you at home for a few days, would you be willing to try it at home?"

"I suppose," she said again.

Charlene Simpson's obesity plagued her for as long as she can remember. In school, relentless teasing occurred at recess. "Fatty, fatty two by four, can't get through the bathroom door," the kids would scream at the top of their lungs. Even today, the thought of the constant teasing would drive her to tears. She tried every diet known to man. The effect resulted in the same disappointing weight loss. She lost up to 100 lbs at one point, but the weight returned over the next 6 months. She rationalized that there must be a medical explanation. After many tests, she discovered her genes determined the predisposition to obesity. She would have to manage a 900-kcal diet for the rest of her life. Having three children in a row caused her weight to surge to over 300 lbs. Because of the rapid weight gain, she developed diabetes, sleep apnea and hypertension. Her family doctor said she would die at a youthful age from the medical conditions complicated by severe obesity.

Meeting Dr. Jeremy Young gave her renewed hope that she would conquer obesity. The reviews online described a careful and empathetic surgeon. He exuded confidence, and she trusted him. When he spoke with her, he explained that obesity resulted from something impossible to control on her own. He explained to her that the genetic design of her body caused obesity. This might have been a survival advantage in the early days of human development. In today's world of plentiful nutrition, having those genes cursed her with a life of obesity. Dr. Young explained that only surgery cured obesity. For the first time in her life, she experienced someone who understood her. Finally, a doctor who took the time to listen and not blame her for eating too much. She readily agreed to have gastric bypass surgery.

Dr. Young stopped at the nursing station and spoke with the discharge planner. "Mrs. Simpson, in room 1506, is reluctant to go home. The reason is that she has three small children, and she's worried she won't get enough rest. Is there any way to organize help at home for her for a day or two? This would allow her to discharge for today."

The discharge planner, used to having this conversation with patients, sympathized with the patient because she understood what it meant to have small children at home and be unable to rest. The discharge planner wanted these doctors to spend the day looking after three toddlers rather than spend all their time at work. That way, they might empathize with the hardships of raising small children. "I'll see what I can do," she snapped back at Dr. Young.

The sharpness of her response surprised Dr. Young, but

because of the early hour of the morning, perhaps she had not yet consumed her morning coffee. Something else in her life might cause her to be in an unpleasant mood. This being of no concern to him, he completed the charting and wrote the discharge orders for the four patients.

While getting ready to leave the nursing station, Jeremy heard the intercom blast, "Code Blue, room 1506. Code Blue, room 1506" It took a millisecond for him to realize that the intercom directed the cardiac arrest team to the room of Charlene Simpson. Jeremy jumped in to help. He took over for the cardiac massage and began pumping her chest. The ICU doctor in charge of the team in the room said, "Everyone stands back. I'm going to defibrillate." By applying the paddles to her chest, the electric current discharged. Her body jumped about one inch from the bed and then settled back on the bed. The ICU doctor repeated the process of defibrillation four times. Charlene had developed the lethal condition of electrical-mechanical dissociation. This is when the heart exhibits electrical activity, but the blood circulation does not occur. Cardiac massage and ventilation continued after the anesthesiologist intubated her. After pumping in adrenaline, other stimulants, and four ampules of bicarbonate, nothing seemed to work. After 30 minutes of resuscitation, with no signs of heart activity, they stopped the cardiac massage. She died. They had nothing further to offer her. The ventilation ceased, and the ICU doctor pronounced her dead at 0700hs.

The tragedy shattered Dr. Young. He talked with her briefly before the cardiac arrest announcement, and she seemed fine. It did not seem possible for this to happen. He performed the gastric bypass surgical procedure perfectly. Her ability to look after three small children at home caused her only concerns about discharge from the hospital. He needed to call the husband and talk to him. The first call he placed to the coroner's office. He spoke with the chief medical examiner and explained, "The surgery procedure proceeded uneventfully with no difficulties. I do not understand how a cardiac arrest occurred. An autopsy to determine the cause of death might clear up why she died so suddenly?"

The chief medical examiner promised to call him after the autopsy in a few days.

Mr. Simpson answered the phone on the second ring. "Mr. Simpson, this is Dr. Young. There is no easy way to tell you this, but your wife suffered a cardiac arrest this morning and died. I am not sure what happened. After speaking with her at 6:30 this morning, I left the room. The cardiac arrest occurred 2 minutes later. She seemed fine when we discussed discharge. I am so sorry."

Initially, nothing but quiet filled the void of the phone line. "Mr. Simpson, are you there?"

"Noooo," Mr. Simpson wailed. "That is not possible! There must be a mistake! She was perfectly healthy. I cannot believe this is happening." Dr. Young heard him weeping at the end of the line. Dr. Young's heart broke at hearing the agonizing grief from the other side of the phone. He only imagined how awful it would be to get this terrible news over the phone.

A bit choked up, Dr. Young said, "The coroner is involved and will try to piece together what happened. I have spoken to him directly. He is going to perform an autopsy to determine why she died. I will call you back in a day or so to see if you have questions. I am so sorry." The conversation ended amid the uncontrollable sobbing at the end of the line.

Another phone call informed the hospital's CEO about the tragic death. The CEO, an early riser, typically arrived at the hospital at 6 AM every morning. Jeremy said. "Jerry, an unexpected death occurred following an uneventful gastric bypass. I saw her two minutes before cardiac arrest, and she seemed fine. We discussed discharge planning. I arranged for the discharge planner to offer help at home to manage the three small children. She suddenly arrested and died. I have asked the coroner to see if an autopsy might determine the cause of death."

"You must be very upset," Jerry said. "Can you come to my office to discuss this further?"

"I will be right up," Jeremy replied.

Chapter 5

Jeremy arrived on the third floor at the CEO's office. It surprised him to see the Chief of Staff and Robert Planter, the chief of psychiatry, sitting at the meeting table in the CEO's office.

"We were just talking about you when you called," said Jerry. "We discussed the medical advisory committee meeting where you brought forward your concerns about the behavior of Dr. Julian Yacoby. Robert explained to me the discussion upset you to the where you stormed out of the meeting before they arrived at a resolution. Robert felt that Julian's punishment of closing the operating room was unjust. Instead, you should be more sympathetic to our surgeons' stresses in these troubling times."

"I would not say I stormed out. The discussion was heading in an illogical direction, so I packed my things quietly and left. I realized early in the discussion that my point of view would not come across to the chiefs in a way that made sense to them. The behavior of Dr. Yacoby is deeply disturbing. My belief remains that there is something terribly wrong with him. His unreturned phone messages prevented me from asking the questions I needed to ask."

Jerry replied. "You do not need to contact him. Robert has taken that upon himself. Robert cannot discuss what is going on as it would breach patient confidentiality. Most of the chiefs agree you overstepped your authority as chief of surgery to shut down his operating room. I agree with them. You must be more sympathetic to the members of your department rather than always going by the strict policy. We need to think about strategies to keep our excellent surgeons, and closing the operating room is not a strategy with which I would agree."

"What's the point of having policies if we don't follow them" retorted Jeremy. "Every year, when we re-apply for privileges, we all agree to abide by the policies and procedures of the hospital, and this is an obvious example. The policy states that physicians will treat all staff respectfully and with dignity. Dr. Yacoby failed to do this. His behavior threatened the nursing staff, who do not want to work with him."

"There's something else I want to talk to you about," said Jerry. "One of our biggest donors, Ron Higgins, called me. He is the chief racing officer from last night. He witnessed the accident near your boat. The concern he raised about the way you managed your boat is worrisome. He alleges your inactions caused another boat's collision and considerable damage resulted. Only blind luck resulted in no one being injured. He alleges you acted irresponsibly. The avoidable accident followed because you insisted you maintain your right of way. Diversion to avoid the accident would have been the sensible option.

"Now you tell me that one of your gastric bypass patients

died. No gastric bypass deaths have happened for the past five years. All this leads me to believe there is something wrong with you, Jeremy, not the other way around."

The room became silent.

"Jeremy, I will ask you to step back as chief of surgery and as a surgeon voluntarily while we investigate the cause of her death. I hope it will give you some time to reflect upon your inflexible attitude and abuse of power as chief of surgery. We should have preliminary results from the coroner's office within a week, and we can meet again afterward."

The total shock caused Jeremy to stare at the CEO. His eyes drifted to the others in the room as they looked down at the table to prevent eye contact with him. His actions toward closing the operation originated from his promise to the nursing staff to provide a safe work environment. Yet the CEO asked him to step back. The chief of staff remained silent during the entire conversation. He neither offered support nor condemned his actions. For one of the few times in his life, Jeremy said nothing. He realized the forces conspiring against him impeded him from effectively performing his job as chief. He spent his entire professional career doing the right thing and treating people with respect and dignity. His colleagues respected and liked him. They told him he treated them fairly. His patients loved and evaluated him with 5-star ratings on the *Rate your doctor* website. Until this time, all his favorable performance reviews allowed him to function effectively as chief. This blow to his professional reputation created damage that might be insurmountable. His face became red, and if he said anything, he would regret it later. He stood up from his chair, turned around, and walked out of the office without closing the door.

He sat in his car for about 15 minutes to settle down his shaking. Jeremy remained visibly upset, angry, and confused. He did not understand how all these things happened to him simultaneously. Jeremy focused on the simple goal of driving home to talk to his wife. He had to get her understanding of what had happened. She started work at around 9:00 AM. The current time of 8:00 AM flashed on his car clock. He ought to get at least 30 minutes of good advice before she starts her day. He drove the 15 minutes home slowly to collect his thoughts.

Chapter 6

To describe Jeremy's wife, Iona, as beautiful would understate how she would light up any room she entered. Her hair, the color of foxtail red, flowed gently over her soft shoulders. Although 2 years younger than Jeremy, she looked at least 10 years younger than her age. She practiced psychotherapy as her area of expertise. Her patients loved her and described her as brilliant. Jeremy depended on her for advice and to keep him headed in the right direction. He had already updated her about the medical advisory committee fiasco and the sailing collision. The complacent and poor attitude of the medical advisory committee shocked her. Patients treated unfairly by bosses who did not follow policies and rules comprised much of her psychotherapy practice. Having no sympathy for Dr. Yacoby, she understood the nurse, who said she worked in an unsafe environment. No sympathy came from Iona for the J35 skipper when he failed to accept responsibility for the damage caused by not following the racing rules.

Jeremy first met Iona in medical school. Iona studied medicine in the class two years behind him, but he immediately noticed her. She was as beautiful now as she was then. Something special about her caused Jeremy's pulse to race the same way, even today. He found her irresistible. The way she walked, the way she would flick her hair when she laughed, the way her eyes would dart around the room and then the way her eyes would eventually lock on his. *"Everything about her was so feminine"* described her best. He thought about her constantly but was too timid to invite her out. Besides, the lack of cash made him insecure that a date might empty his bank account. She looked a few levels up on the student socioeconomic scale. He worried that a date night would be expensive. The main reason for his trepidation to inquire about a date was it terrified him that her response would be no.

On weekends in the summer, Jeremy and his friends would race sailboats. They rarely won. They enjoyed the excitement and the competitiveness, especially at the start of the race. Racing sailboats gave them a distraction from studying and school life. On one of the race Saturdays, Chip Ramsey, the sailboat's skipper, invited Iona.

Chip hailed from a family of surgeons, all excellent sailors. They raced on a C&C 30 sailboat. Chip, handsome and tall at 6'2", studied at Rotman's School of Business. He professed to be an entrepreneur. He boasted that his goal of becoming a millionaire by thirty followed his family's tradition of establishing enormous wealth at a young age. A perfect match for someone as exquisite as Iona. They composed his racing team of five other male sailors, including Jeremy and, for today, Iona, the sole woman on board.

The ten-knot wind made for perfect sailboat racing. Out of

the three races, they came 2nd last in 2 of the races. On the last race, thanks to a lucky wind shift, they crossed the finish line first. The surprise for the sailors on Chip's boat generated a lot of hooting and hollering. The racing team members hugged and slapped each other on the back. When Jeremy came to hug Iona, the hug lasted longer than Jeremy expected. When he attempted to kiss her on the cheek like the other sailors, Jeremy's lips landed on Iona's lips. She parted her lips, and her tongue slipped into Jeremy's mouth. Jeremy's pulse raced. Avoiding passing out in the ecstasy that coursed through his body required all his concentration. Jeremy sat down to prevent this from happening after the prolonged kiss finished. Iona smiled at him. No one else seemed to notice.

Later, in the clubhouse, drinking beer, Jeremy and Iona chatted incessantly. For them, no one else appeared to be in the room. They focused their attention only on each other. At one point, Chip interrupted, offering Iona a ride home, but she declined, saying she would find her way home. Jeremy and Iona lingered there until the server informed them the clubhouse was closed after midnight, so they had to depart. No one else remained in the clubhouse. Their long and happy relationship started on that day. When they reflected on that first magical encounter in the following years, they believed on that day; they truly found their soul mate in each other.

Jeremy thought of that first encounter driving home from the hospital. It helped that Iona would be at home. His depressed thoughts caused him to have trouble focusing. Iona would have the answers to his many questions. Upon entering the house, he found Iona in the kitchen, drinking coffee and eating a peanut butter bagel. Jeremy sat down across from her and sipped on the cup of coffee she had prepared for him. He filled her in about the events of the morning. He explained the death of the gastric bypass patient. This was followed by a disastrous meeting with the CEO, chief of staff, and chief of psychiatry and his "voluntary" suspension. Any ideas about what to do next escaped Jeremy.

"The first thing you need to do," Iona said, "is to call your medical protective agency. The treatment is unacceptable and incredibly unfair. You will require strong legal advice. You have always done the right thing and maintained the highest of principles. They have turned this around against you. We will prepare to fight this. Although it is unclear what's going on, at some stage, it will all come out."

Jeremy spent the rest of the day typing notes about what transpired and speaking with his protective medical lawyer, Marco. By the time evening rolled around, he believed things had improved. Jeremy put things into perspective and came around to believe that he did nothing wrong. He convinced himself everything would work out in the end. He reflected on his luck as he lay in bed with his wife snuggled against his chest, softly breathing in a deep sleep. Although the answers failed to be clear about why his professional world fell apart, Iona supported him. She took care of him during the challenging times. Iona often told him she loved him unconditionally and would do so until the end. She always provided a happy and safe home. Jeremy believed loving such a wonderful woman made him a better man.

Chapter 7

"There are toxic levels of remifentanil in her blood," said the coroner over the phone to Jeremy a few days later. "I believe the cause of death is respiratory failure secondary to these toxic levels."

"Are you sure?" Said Jeremy incredulously. "I would never prescribe remifentanil to our postoperative patients. The only time we use it at our hospital is for the anesthesiologist to reduce the dose of propofol that they administer during the operation. The anesthesiologist intubates patients while on a ventilator, so respiratory failure is not an issue in the operating room. It really makes little sense remifentanil turned up in her blood sample. Patients quickly metabolize the drug, and it is out of the bloodstream within fifteen minutes. Remifentanil, administered at the time of surgery, would have dissipated from her system by the time the anesthetic was complete."

"We also sent the samples to our provincial lab to confirm this. We are signing this off as a drug overdose. When we have seen this kind of thing before, it is usually a medication error, but we will leave it to the hospital to sort this out. As this is such an extraordinary cause of mortality, there will be an inquest, and we will call upon you to give evidence."

"Anything I can do; I would be happy to help," said Jeremy.

Jeremy sighed an enormous sigh of relief. At least the surgery did not cause her death. The explanation for death resulted from a drug overdose. He videotaped and reviewed his operations with the residents and other surgeons as part of the surgery quality assurance program. That she overdosed on drugs absolved Jeremy of any wrongdoing related to the operation. Either a medication error occurred from the pharmacy or nursing staff, or perhaps she administered it herself. A fentanyl problem in Toronto resulted in people dying from overdoses daily. The narcotic overdose crisis made the news every day. The possibility that she brought the remifentanil herself crossed his mind, or perhaps someone brought it in for her. Jeremy pulled out his phone to discuss with the CEO that the reason for death was an overdose. This vindicated him. Then the doorbell rang.

Jeremy answered the door. Two uniformed police officers stood at the door. One officer said, "You are getting arrested for the murder of Mrs. Charlene Simpson. We are charging you with first-degree murder. I must inform you that you may retain and instruct Counsel in private without delay. You may call any lawyer you want." The officer placed handcuffs on his wrists and ushered him into the police car. The arrest happened so quickly that the shock of the event, although unsettling, did not register with Jeremy until the cruiser sped away from his house.

The darkness in the jail cell spooked Jeremy. The faint

aroma of bleach, urine, and human sweat that permeated the air made him nauseous. Jeremy tried to make sense of the events. The humiliation of being photographed, fingerprinted, and locked in the small 8 by 8-foot cell sank him into despair. News reporters and cameras screamed at him when he arrived at the police station. Jeremy tried to hide his face, a futile endeavor as the cameras flashed all around him. They would plaster his picture over social media and news outlets. He feared they would judge him before he cleared his name. The police advised him not to say anything until he spoke with his lawyer. He phoned Marco and the lawyer provided to him by the medical protective insurance group. Marco, on his way down to the station, explained that he should be there within the hour. He assured him he would clear everything up, as there must have been a huge mistake. That phone call to Marco occurred six hours ago. Frustrated, Jeremy waited in the damp and cold cell.

A short while later, he heard footsteps coming down the hallway. Two police officers unlocked the door and again placed tight handcuffs on him. The police officers said, "Come with us, please."

They took Jeremy into a small room with two chairs on each side of a table. The two men removed the handcuffs and told Jeremy to wait. Within a few minutes, two men walked into the room. "Hello, Dr. Young. I am Marco, the lawyer assigned to you by the medical protective insurance group. We spoke on the phone. This is

Michael, one of my associates."

Jeremy, filled with anger, paced the room like a caged lion. His blood pressure sky-rocketed, about ready to boil over. With his face red, as his pulse raced, he asked in a loud voice, "I don't understand what is happening. Can you enlighten me? This is turning out to be one of the worst days of my life, and I have never been so humiliated."

Marco said, "The police have arrested you because they believe you administered remifentanil to Charlene Simpson. They allege this resulted in respiratory arrest and caused her death. We will review some reasons that led to their conclusions in a bit, but we want you to understand that we are here to help you. The medical protective insurance agency only covers medical malpractice. They charged you with a criminal offense, first-degree murder, so I asked Michael, one of the top criminal lawyers in the country, for his help. You must pay for your own defense. I will let Michael explain what will happen from here."

Michael spoke. "First, I would like to say how sorry this has happened to you. I do not have all the details yet, but I will fill you in as I get them. I will hold anything that you say in complete confidence. Before we start, I think you should understand that I have successfully defended similar cases and will use any means to clear this up. For me to defend you, I will have to ask you to sign these papers, which gives me the authority to be your attorney. As far as legal fees, I expect this to be quite expensive, and I'm going to ask for a $200,000 retainer, and I expect, after everything, this to be closer to $500,000. If you are OK with this, you can sign right here."

Jeremy became overwhelmed. All he thought about centered on the unreal series of events and that this could not be happening to him. After signing the papers, the lawyers encouraged him to recount in his own words what had happened over the past few days. Jeremy told of his encounter with Mrs. Simpson from when he met with her in the office, the conduct of the surgery, and the first postoperative visit the following day. He said, "How she ended up with toxic levels of remifentanil in her blood, causing her death, mystifies me as I never prescribe that drug."

"Here's the thing," said Michael. "There are 1600 video cameras in the hospital. There are no video cameras inside the patient's room for patient confidentiality, but they are in the hallways. The nurse seen on video entered room 1506 at 3:00 AM to administer the blood thinners. You entered the room next at 6:30 AM. At 6:35 AM, Charlene Simpson suffered from cardiac arrest and subsequently died."

"Have you considered the possibility that she administered the remifentanil to herself?" asked Jeremy.

Michael pointed out, "They strictly managed remifentanil. The only access to this is through the hospital pharmacy. People can buy Fentanyl on the street. Remifentanil is ten times as potent as fentanyl. There has never been a death from a remifentanil overdose in Toronto until Charlene Simpson. As chief of surgery, the hospital administrators allege that you would have access to remifentanil. They claim you have the means of overcoming the checks and balances, so there would be no alarms alerted when some of it disappeared."

"That is ridiculous," exclaimed Jeremy. "I have no more access to remifentanil than you do. I do not know how to get it, let alone administer it, as I have never used it on patients."

"There's something else that implicates you as a suspect in causing her death," said Michael. "The police found 30 doses of remifentanil hidden in your car."

Chapter 8

Julian Yacoby sat in his car opposite the precinct as the darkness of the evening replaced the sunny afternoon. The warm evening brought out crowds of city dwellers eager to enjoy the city's nightlife. He had been sitting in the car for the past 4 hours, thinking and planning. Springtime arrived in Toronto. Although the precinct rested on a side street, the pedestrians swarmed the roads and sidewalks, gnarling the heavy Toronto traffic. Small groups of young adults talked and laughed, happy to be outside after the frigid winter, as they headed to the outdoor restaurants. Julian watched them as they walked by the car. An occasional vehicle passed Julian's car, but the heavily tinted windows made him invisible to the outside world.

Julian wanted to make sure of a few things before he made his next move. Julian understood that Jeremy Young strived on his reputation of being a good person and a skillful administrator, and certainly one not to cross. He kept track of his performance during the past few years. Julian strategized how he might use Jeremy's situation to his advantage. It would all come down to execution and timing, something at which he has recently become remarkably skilled. However, the stress of everything came through as these uncontrolled outbursts.

Julian concluded Jeremy pegged him as a problem that

needed to be managed. Julian accepted Jeremy was right, thinking there was something wrong with him. A straightforward solution for Julian's problem would not materialize easily. Until recently, Julian successfully hid his problem from Jeremy. Julian lived with and managed his problem in his own way. The last few years proved difficult. Julian was a drug addict. His drug of choice now is cocaine. As a teenager, he became the "go-to" for marijuana in high school. Julian became known for his quality products and kept customers returning with his competitive prices. He fell deeper into his addiction as he went through medical school and his surgical training. He discovered cocaine. It took him until recently to acknowledge this had developed into a severe problem. Accepting his cocaine addiction became a key turning point in teaching him how best to manage it and turn the addiction into a benefit.

Julian tried cutting himself off cocaine early in his orthopedic surgery residency by visiting a deserted island in the Bahamas. He rented a small sailboat by himself and stocked up for a week's supply of food and water in Nassau before sailing due south for fifty miles. Julian anchored off Shroud Cay in a deserted bay of brilliant blue water. He desperately hoped that the isolation, sun, and natural beauty would trick his brain into understanding that in life, beauty and wonder dominated the world. That might trigger dopamine release and get him off the cocaine. That withdrawal strategy lasted a mere thirty-six sleepless hours before he pulled up the anchor and headed back to Nassau. He had a contact in Nassau and scored enough crack cocaine to help relieve the terrible dysphoria which resulted from not having the drug in his system. It would be hopeless to get off the stuff.

While in medical school, he did an extra rotation on psychiatry and worked with a neurophysiologist. He researched how cocaine depletes dopamine. He discovered how it becomes an addiction where the cravings never disappear completely. In rare circumstances, an addict can learn to live without cocaine, but only after much pain and suffering. Cocaine causes an increase in dopamine release in the brain. Dopamine is the natural chemical in the brain that leads to pleasant sensations of satisfaction and happiness. The genetic predisposition to a reduction in the levels of dopamine receptors causes cocaine addiction. Addicts need that extra jolt of dopamine just to feel "normal." Julian fell into this category. Cocaine made him feel "normal." Julian learned that over time and with repeated use, the brain adapts to excess dopamine. This reduces the effects of cocaine. Increasing amounts of the drug are necessary to avoid the onset of withdrawal symptoms, such as depression and insomnia. He long ago accepted that cocaine addiction plagued his everyday life and carefully planned to manage this. Lately, however, the addiction caught up to him. He tried to cut back on his use of cocaine, but this only resulted in these terrible outbursts in the operating room and on the surgical floor.

Julian reached into the glove compartment and pulled out his cocaine kit. He carefully placed a small line of 100% cocaine and snorted the contents into his left nostril. Within seconds, the drug kicked in. As the drug entered his system, the negative thoughts quickly disappeared. A smile drifted across his face as he rationalized everything would work out. Julian had come this far, medical school, residency, and 5 years of exceptional surgical practice, and no one even suspected his cocaine addiction. He planned to take complete control thanks to his deception, expertise, and ruthless determination. He had kept his secret safe all these years...... except for Jeremy Young, who had uncovered that Julian had something to hide. Julian would see Jeremy Young's destruction in the interest of self-preservation.

Chapter 9

She barricaded Julian, only ten years old, in the closet he hated. His mother forcibly threw him there in the morning. The night was approaching, and the only light that entered the tiny room was diminishing. This light came from the narrow slit at the bottom of the door. Crying would only make his mother angry, but he couldn't help himself.

She would not discover the tears running down his cheeks until she freed him. He learned from a painful experience that his mother would prolong his punishment if he shouted or asked to be let out. He tried to be as quiet as possible. It smelled of urine and feces in the closet. Before his mother let him go to bed, this mess needed to be cleaned if she released him tonight.

The school was the only place where he found safety. He discovered the learning part came easily, and his teachers told him they recognized him as one of the brightest students in the school. He would sneak into the library during recess to learn about animal anatomy. Julian had no interest in playing tag or skipping rope with the other children.

His father had left over a year ago, never to return. He brought home a small golden lab puppy. Julian named the puppy "Lucky" because it was the only time his father had given him anything. His father said he must leave town for a while and needed someone to take care of his friend's puppy until he returned. Julian's father left with his new friend and never came back. His mother blamed Julian for his father running off with his girlfriend and leaving them. That is when the closet punishment began.

Anatomy fascinated Julian. As the puppy grew up, he would scratch his belly as Lucky rolled over on his back. Julian liked to palpate the liver and other organs, attempting to identify the names of the internal organs. The books in the library helped. One day, he took Lucky into the shed. While scratching his belly, the puppy's eyes lovingly looked at Julian. He pulled out his father's hunting knife and slit the puppy's throat. A gurgling sound resulted from air bubbling through the open windpipe as the puppy tried to wiggle away from Julian. Julian held him tight until Lucky stopped moving. The blood spewed like a fountain everywhere from the open carotid arteries, much more than he ever expected. When Lucky stopped moving, he used the knife to open the abdomen. Julian removed the organs individually, leaving the intestines until the last. He opened the chest and removed the heart. It fascinated him. He relished sensations of power and control for the first time.

He cleaned up the mess, washed his clothes in the washing machine, and buried Lucky and some organs in the backyard. His mother would be returning from her server job at the local tavern later in the evening, so she would never find out what happened. Julian placed the liver, spleen, and heart in individual vodka-filled jars he had stolen from the liquor cabinet. He hid the jars behind empty buckets on a shelf in the shed.

He did not question his mother when she failed to ask the whereabouts of Lucky. Julian returned to the shed and removed the organs to re-live the dissection process at least once a week until the organs deteriorated. When the organs had completely liquefied and were no longer removable, he threw the jars into the garbage.

Chapter 10

Julian noted the two well-dressed men in dark suits walk into the precinct. He followed them inside. Casually looking at the men's wanted posters in the lobby, he listened to their conversation. He picked up a pamphlet on preventing auto theft while they spoke with the duty officer. He heard them explain they were the lawyers acting on behalf of Dr. Jeremy Young and that they needed to meet with him. They had ushered the lawyers inside and sat in a closed-off office. Julian saw them through the glass walls but, not hearing the conversations, left the precinct.

Julian returned to his car to plan his next steps. Surprised they had taken so long, Julian quietly remained in the car. When they left, many hours later, the time came for him to make his move. Julian waited until the "suits" had passed his car, then walked into the precinct to talk with the same duty officer.

"My name is Dr. Julian Yacoby, and I am here to see Dr. Jeremy Young," he said.

"Is he a guest here?" the duty officer said, smiling at his wit. He used two fingers to type on his keypad of the computer. He found the information he sought. "Ah, I see. What do you want with him? Are you a family member? There are visiting hours which are between 9-11 every morning. You are going to have to wait until then."

"Dr. Young is a surgeon at the Metropolitan Hospital. I must speak with him about patient care issues. They arrested him suddenly, and he did not have time to hand off the patients. This is a matter of life and death. I will only be a few minutes. I must ask him questions only he can answer. Surely you understand the importance of patient care and how disruptive this arrest is for the hospital."

The duty officer looked at Julian, not sure what to say. Certain that the duty officer had never had to deal with a situation like this, Julian gave him time to think. After a few seconds, the duty officer said, "Give me a minute."

Julian watched him go into one of the glassed offices to speak with another of the officers. After a few minutes, he returned and said to Julian, "Follow me."

They led Julian into what appeared to be an interrogation room. He sat down at a table opposite him; another chair remained vacant. The expected one-way mirror on the wall positioned on the left side of the room reflected Julian's image. Julian suspected the hidden microphones in the room would record their private conversation. After about 10 minutes, the door opened, and the officers ushered Jeremy Young into the room. He sat down opposite Julian. An astonished expression from Jeremy revealed his shock at seeing him there. The surprise on Jeremy's face revealed the reaction Julian hoped to see.

Julian said, "I would first like to apologize for our last interaction. You were 100% correct in stopping the operating room to investigate my inappropriate outburst. I came here today to see what I need to do to help you. Jerry, our CEO, has asked me to be the interim chief of surgery until your legal situation gets resolved. I told him that before I accepted, I wanted to discuss this with you. I also want to find out if there were any medical care issues that you wanted me to transfer to one of the other general surgeons."

Jeremy said, "Honestly, Julian, you were the last person I would have expected to see here. I am shocked that you would take it upon yourself to help me. I currently have no patients in the hospital regarding transferring any medical issues. I accept your apologies, and I accept your offer of help. If you think you can be chief of surgery while I get my situation sorted out, I will do whatever I can to help you."

Julian said, "Thanks Jeremy, this means a lot to me."

The conversation continued with questions from Julian. He asked about the conditions inside the prison. Julian offered to bring anything to Jeremy that might make his day less uncomfortable. They discussed the tragic and unexpected gastric bypass death and the remifentanil finding in Jeremy's car. Jeremy said, "I have never used that drug on any patients, and I do not know how to access it. I do not understand how it ended up in my car."

"Do not worry about any of that stuff for now. I have 100% confidence that there is a rational reason to explain that. I am certain we will get this mess sorted out soon. I would also like to offer you bail support if it comes to that. I can put up a $1,000,000 bond if needed. I am sure you have done nothing wrong, and I will do whatever I can to help you," said Julian.

After ten more minutes of discussion, they bid each other farewell and good luck. The guards accompanied Jeremy back to his jail cell, and Julian made his way to the car.

Jeremy lay on his bunk in jail, trying to understand what had just happened. Jeremy experienced tough times in his 57 years, but never as awful a time as he lives through now. He understood it would be hard to grasp everything that had occurred and make sense of anything. Julian coming to visit just added to the confusion in his mind. This made absolutely no sense. He knew with certainty that there was something wrong with Julian. Jeremy succeeded as chief of surgery for over 2 years because of his accurate intuition. Jeremy's sixth sense never failed to identify these problems. Julian's bizarre behavior defied explanation and continued to occupy his thoughts. The unexpected generosity flabbergasted Julian. This generosity seemed completely out of character. All Jeremy could do was go with the flow and see where it took him. He drifted in and out of sleep, often waking up disoriented before remembering he was in jail and then going back to sleep.

Chapter 11

"All rise," said the court registrar.

Jeremy stood in the prisoner's dock of the courthouse as he watched the judge walk in to sit behind the bench. The judge looked to be 75 years old and appeared annoyed. He wore a black robe and walked with a slight limp. His wrinkled face and disheveled gray hair portrayed a life of late nights and double martini lunches. A look of displeasure swept over his face as he peered toward Jeremy, then glanced at the papers on the desk.

The crown attorney and Michael both bowed their heads, acknowledging the judge. "You may sit," said the court registrar after the judge sat down. The room remained silent as the judge shuffled the papers, then selected one and read it to himself. After 2 minutes, the judge looked up at Jeremy and said, "They have charged you with first-degree murder. This is a bail hearing."

Michael stood. "We would like Jeremy to be released on bail," said Michael. "He is a respected surgeon in the community. He is not a flight risk. The evidence presented against him is flimsy and circumstantial."

Standing up, the crown attorney said, "The charges of first-degree murder against him are serious. We believe he is best kept in jail on tertiary grounds until the court date. The public must have faith and confidence in the judicial system. Allowing him out on bail weakens the judicial process. We have a powerful case against him and expect a conviction that would imprison him with no parole for 25 years."

Michael stood. "This is the first time they have brought any charges like this against my client. Dr. Young is of no risk to the public. He will not work at the hospital or see patients until he is cleared of all charges. He has agreed not to discuss the case with any witnesses and will remain confined to Ontario until the trial."

The judge glared at the two lawyers. "I'm going to have a short recess while I decide what to do".

"All rise," said the court registrar.

Michael conferred with Jeremy. "The Judge is reviewing the case and evidence in his chambers. The Judge usually sets bail at a high enough amount that most clients cannot pay in cases like this. I would expect bail to be $500,000-$1 million. Do you think you could come up with that amount of money?"

Jeremy said, "A surgeon at my hospital offered to place up to $1 million. I'm uncertain about what I should do. If I accept his offer, it may put me in an awkward situation." Jeremy explained to Michael his concerns about Julian's bizarre behavior.

"At some point, in my role as chief of surgery, I might have to discipline him. I am uncertain about what is wrong with him, but I am hesitant to put myself in a situation where it would be tough for me to 'do the right thing' if it ever came to that."

Michael looked at Jeremy incredulously. "They charge you with first-degree murder, and you are concerned about 'doing the right thing'? You need to think about yourself. You will not do well stuck in prison trying to clear your name. My advice is to take his offer and deal with any repercussions at a later stage."

As Jeremy contemplated the words coming from Michael, the court registrar entered the courtroom and said, "All rise."

The judge entered and sat down behind the bench. "I have made my decision," he said. "Balancing the scales of justice is never easy. The court must remain fair and impartial. While I agree that the risk to the public and the flight risk is low, the first-degree murder charge is serious. However, the first principle for any defendant is innocent until proven guilty. I'm going to set bail at $1,000,000. I adjourn this courtroom."

"All rise," said the court registrar. The judge walked out of the courtroom.

Chapter 12

Three days later, Jeremy sat in the kitchen at his home. The morning sun lit up the room while he drank coffee with Iona. They attempted to assemble the pieces of what had transpired over the past few days. After a quick court appearance, his lawyer, Michael, pushed for his release from jail, and the judge agreed to set bail. As promised, the $1 million bail rendered by Julian raised more questions than answers for Jeremy. They appointed Julian as interim chief of surgery at the hospital, while they advised Jeremy to stay on a voluntary leave of absence. His lawyer advised Jeremy not to contact anyone at the hospital and to stay indoors as much as possible. Michael advised him not to talk to any press or accept any interviews on TV for any reason.

"So," said Iona, "let us make a chart of everything known and the other parts that remain a mystery. We will do it on an Excel spreadsheet."

They made separate headings, including Julian, Sailing incident, Medical Advisory fiasco, Gastric bypass death, remifentanil, the Murder charge, and Legal battle. Under each heading, they listed when the events had occurred with a timeline. They printed off the sheets and placed them on the wall in the study. The arrows pointed to different groupings and back to where the events intersected. They composed a list of questions. They grouped the questions in terms of urgency. Jeremy and Iona planned to update these lists every 24 hours. Jeremy's anxiety improved as he recorded these thoughts on paper. He needed to be in control, and visualizing the events on paper helped him cope. He clarified the picture and his understanding of how they were interconnected by writing everything down. The related events showed up connected with arrows. Iona, the most organized person he had ever met, brought value and order to his life.

Jeremy said, "The most pressing question for me is how did that remifentanil end up in Charlene Sinclair? Analyzing the videos for the night, they saw the nurse walk into the room to give blood thinners at around 3:00 in the morning. I entered at 6:30 at the crack of dawn. Nobody else entered the room for the entire night. When I stepped into the room, I did not spot anyone else in the room either."

"What I would suggest," said Iona, "is the first thing to do would be to review those videos yourself. There must be an explanation. I would trust no one in this medical facility at this point."

"How will I do that if I can't go into the hospital?" asked Jeremy.

"I have an idea," said Iona. "Let me make a phone call."

Three hours later, Jeremy positioned himself in front of his computer. He loaded a copy of the video from that night to early morning, showing Charlene Simpson's room. Iona, her usual incredible self, got the videos. One of Iona's psychotherapy patients worked on the IT team at the hospital. Iona assured Jeremy that no one would trace the video back to him or to her patient. Iona kept what she said to her patient to get the video to herself. Jeremy was astoundingly grateful for the opportunity to peruse the videos. Jeremy, an expert at reviewing videos, developed the skill during his surgical career. For the past 25 years, he videotaped every operation he performed. Whenever a problem or concern arose post-operatively, he would look at the video and see if an explanation would be visible on inspection. Jeremy wanted to learn from what mistakes happened at the surgery to avoid repeating the mistake at another operation. At other times, he would scrutinize the operation conducted by a resident, and he would identify even the smallest errors. He would then provide sensible counsel on how to enhance the surgical technique. He planned to draw on his expertise from reviewing videos after all those years to find something the security team had missed in the videos.

He ran the videos at 2 X regular speed but would speed it up when nothing obvious turned up in the video. Jeremy was determined to watch all 12 hours of video, and so far, nothing seemed out of the ordinary. At 0300h, the nurse entered the room to give the anticoagulation. The nurse exited the room at 0305h. Jeremy dismissed the concept that the nurse furnished the remifentanil. The drug takes fewer than 60 seconds to act, and the patient did not have cardiac arrest until 0635h.

Jeremy spent the next six hours going frame by frame from 0306h to 0635h. At the 0530-time mark, he thought he had spotted something. It almost seemed there was a pale shadow drifting toward room 1506. Even though he wasn't a believer in ghosts, it appeared ghostlike. It seemed to blend in with the color of the walls. He saw this because he stopped the video to refill his coffee cup. When he returned from the kitchen, he noted that the video had stopped between two frames. Looking at the side of the frame, he spotted a slight difference in the beige color of the wall. The texture also seemed slightly coarser. He slowly advanced the frames and noted that this 'shadow' seemed to enter room 1506. He advanced the video to where he stepped into the room at 0630h and when left at 0633h. At around the 0634h time mark, he slowed down the video. Again, he moved frame by frame and saw a similar 'shadow' that seemed to exit room 1506.

"Iona," he yelled, "Come and see this!"

Iona came racing up the study stairs and sat beside Jeremy. He reviewed his video findings with her before he showed her the 'shadow'. He moved the frames back and forth ten times to make his point.

"Well," he said. "What do you think? "

"Honey," she said. "There is nothing there. I think you are seeing things in your desperation to find something. There are so many plausible explanations for your so-called 'shadow.' Perhaps there was a slight breeze drifting by when someone opened a door down the hallway, causing a bit of dust to be disturbed. An electrical disturbance or slight vibration in the video camera would cause a disturbance in the image. There really is nothing there, honey….."

Sensing his profound disappointment, she said, "Keep looking. You'll come across something. I am certain that you will find an explanation."

Iona's comments caused Jeremy to hang his head on his chest. At first, he directed his disappointment toward Iona for not seeing what he saw in the videos. Then Jeremy directed the disappointment at himself. Iona pointed out that in his desperation to find something in the videos, he likely saw things that were not there. He spent the next 15 minutes reviewing the videos again. He reviewed thousands of videos in the last 25 years, and the more he looked at these videos, the more he became convinced this 'shadow' existed and entered room 1506. Jeremy was certain that Charlene Simpson's unexpected death must have a connection to this 'shadow'.

While he contemplated where he would look next, he returned to the videos sent to him by Iona's patient. She sent videos of all 1600 cameras in a compressed file. Not knowing where to start, he opened the video in the doctor's parking lot. At 0600h, he always arrived first at the medical facility. Parking his car, he saw himself get out and head towards the hospital doorway. He then flipped over to the video of the hospital entrance. Jeremy noted the time when others entered the building. Most nurses would arrive at the hospital at around 0715h for the start of the 0730 shift. He saw himself on video as he entered the hospital at 0601h. Between 0601h and 0634h, only three other people entered. He recognized two as early-morning phlebotomists and the third as an ENT surgeon.

Jeremy sat back in his chair and sighed. This looked hopeless. With over 1600 cameras to review and limited time to review them, he needed to focus on the next step. A thought flashed across his mind. Room 1506 on the 15th floor rested directly across the hallway from the stairs of the fire exit. He quickly found the videotape of the stairway entrance on the main floor. He set the time between 0500h and 0640h. Nobody entered or exited the stairway during that time. He then reviewed the entrance to the stairs from the second-floor video. No one entered or exited. When he looked at the 16th-floor video, at 0525, someone entered the staircase. This person wore a surgical mask, cap, gloves, and a blue scrub suit. The person attempted to avoid the cameras because the head remained low on the chest while moving quickly into the staircase. The difficulty arose in determining whether this person was a man or a woman. Determining the age of the person proved difficult as well. Later, a person, certainly the same one who entered the 16th floor, exited the elevator on the 18th floor at 0635h.

Jeremy froze the frame and examined the video. He guessed this person's height at about 5'8", somewhat stocky, and likely a man. It looked like a 3 CC syringe in the chest pocket when the magnified picture appeared, with a tiny package tucked underneath the right arm. As this person hurried through the video, the image blurred, and the facial features looked unclear. Jeremy moved the frame to the 18th floor as the same person exited. The 3CC syringe in the chest pocket was absent when he zoomed in on the image. There was no bundle beneath the right arm. Whoever was the 'shadow' could have draped a beige-colored sheet to conceal from the cameras. The 'shadow' could have remained concealed in the spacious private bathroom in room 1506 and administered the drug after Jeremy exited the room. Without 'the shadow', anyone would assume Jeremy gave the remifentanil. "Why would anyone do this?" he said out loud to no one.

Jeremy rapidly reproduced these images and stored them in his file under the heading of remifentanil. He would piece together more information before having another discussion with Iona. He couldn't bear the thought of her having the same view of him as when he shared the video of the 'shadow'. It was getting late, and Iona had gone to bed about an hour earlier. Suddenly, intense fatigue seized him. As soon as he laid his head on the pillow, he drifted into a peaceful slumber.

Chapter 13

It was a gorgeous spring morning with the sun beaming as Jeremy headed for a 10-kilometer run. There was dew on his driveway, leaving shoe prints. The spring air cooled his skin, leaving a pleasant sensation. He was wearing shorts and a singlet. Although the run would be cool initially, after 10 minutes, he would work up a sweat. After several minutes of running, his mind would start to evaluate and address many of his issues. Regularly in the past few years, after completing a run, he worked out many of his issues that might have seemed unresolvable before the run. He would try to run every day, not minding if the weather brought rain, sunshine, or even a blizzard. Iona teased him, saying that this running habit turned into an addiction. She would opt for having a glass of wine after a day's work while he would go for a jog. He admitted she was on the right track because he found running irresistibly. On the rare occasions when he did not go on a run on a particular day, he simply would not feel himself. On those days, restlessness and irritability would settle in. Iona would say he was behaving like a trapped beast, and she would send him out of the house for a run. When he returned, all covered with sweat, she would comment, "Ah, that's better."

His run took him past the hospital. The anger burned inside his chest as he glided by the large gray building that had been the source of his grief. His pulse rate sped as anxiety replaced the calm that the running brought. He picked up the pace as if to purge the negativity from his body. His legs burned as he pushed himself harder. The hospital occupied most of the block. By the time he passed it, he had slowed his pace to catch his breath. He had to stop and place his hands on his knees with his head slightly down as the light-headedness caused him to be unsteady. After a minute, he stood up and realized he was standing right in front of the church building next to the hospital. He had not spoken with Reverend Rowen for at least a year. He spotted him in the church's vestibule.

"Jeremy!" yelled Reverend Rowen. "Get over here. It's fantastic to see you!"

Jeremy jogged over to the steps. "It's terrific to see you, too. It has been about a year since I last saw you."

"Sorry to hear about all your troubles, Jeremy. I believe nothing of what they said about you on the news, and I'm here to help you if you need it. It is time for my 5-year colonoscopy, so I need you to get back in action to get that over with."

Jeremy removed the reverend's colon cancer five years earlier. He has seen him yearly since then. He also removed breast cancer from his wife about 15 years before and his eldest daughter's gallbladder two years ago. Every time the reverend came for a visit, he always brought a gift and spent 10 minutes thanking Jeremy for saving his life and the lives of his wife and daughter. His gratitude always appeared genuine and authentic.

"Come inside and have a cup of coffee. Let's chat and see what I can do to help you."

For the next hour, Jeremy spoke about the past week's events. He described the bizarre behavior of Julian. He recounted the medical advisory committee fiasco and the sailing boat accident. The death of his patient resulted in him being charged with murder. The reverend listened with the occasional "Uh huh" and "I see".

After Jeremy finished talking, the reverend said. "That is an amazing story, and for this to happen to you, of all people, is astonishing. As a reverend, I listen to all kinds of stories and keep them secret, but I've never heard such a story in all my experiences. Let me think about how I can help you over the next few days. Here's my cell phone number. Can you call me next Tuesday?"

Jeremy removed his cellular phone and entered the number. He saved it under his contacts. He placed his cell phone on the table.

Upon saying their goodbyes, Jeremy left the church and started jogging. A few minutes later, remembering that he left his cellular phone on the table, Jeremy turned around to get it. He ran up the church's stairs and retrieved his phone from the table. He was about to leave when the thought crossed his mind that the reverend might wonder who picked up the forgotten phone. So that the reverend would not worry that someone else had taken it, Jeremy wanted to alert him. Jeremy tried to call the reverend, but the call went unanswered. The recording stated that the voicemail was full. There was a doorway at the end of the room that he saw the reverend head for when he left. He swung open the door, which went down some stairs. At the bottom of the stairs appeared another door. He pulled open the door, which revealed a long hallway illuminated by dull incandescent light bulbs. He followed the poorly lit hallway.

Jeremy had been a donor to the church for many years. The church suffered from a lack of a constant stream of funds. The reverend tried hard to keep the church afloat. Reverend Rowen had not contacted Jeremy for a donation for at least two years. Jeremy also noted that they constructed the new stonework at the front of the church and new gardens around it. Although beautiful, it also looked very expensive. Two years ago, the reverend brushed this off by saying that the Lord works in mysterious ways. He explained that an enormous sum of money from an anonymous donor resolved the financial problems.

The hallway continued for about 200 meters. It was strange that there would be such a hallway underneath the church. The length of the passage seemed clearly longer than the church itself. Jeremy continued to follow this hallway. When he reached the end, another door opened into a vast room. The room was brightly lit, temporarily blinded Jeremy as he came from the dark hallway. The room, the size of a hockey arena, hosted a hive of activity. Several rows of tables with empty glass bottles connected to copper tubing filled the walls. These tubes led to a maze of pipes at the ceiling. The room housed three large plastic containers at one end. Trays of sheer liquid that bubbled beneath the fume cupboards filled the room's far end. They arranged trays filled with what looked like a white powder in piles at the isolated part of the room. A conveyor belt loaded the powder into plastic wrapping and piled the packages onto the wooden skids.

Jeremy looked around the room incredulously. It became obvious in his disoriented mind that he stumbled upon a colossal drug production facility. Where the heck was the reverend? And how did this involve the church? Although Jeremy had never seen a large-scale drug production operation, this would be how he imagined it would look. Ten people walked around in white hazmat suits and rebreather masks. This was presumably to protect them from the chemicals that spewed from the fumes in the air, not sucked up by the fume cupboards. Jeremy decided on a quick exit. He quickly realized that no one was supposed to see whatever this facility produced under the church. As Jeremy backed up to exit through the door, a needle-like prick jabbed into his neck. His hand grabbed the painful spot by reflex, but it was too late. When he turned around to see what had happened, his consciousness had slipped away. The last image filling his vision was someone in a hazmat suit holding a needle and syringe. The face behind the hazmat suit looked somewhat familiar. His last thought was that it resembled the reverend. He crumpled onto the floor, and he fell into complete blackness.

Chapter 14

Julian paced back and forth in the tiny chief of surgery office at the hospital. He needed to think and develop a plan. Jeremy was becoming a genuine pain in the ass. Of all the luck, how Jeremy ended up stumbling into the factory threw a wrench into his carefully constructed plans. Jeremy witnessed the drug production operation at the most inopportune time. Julian needed just two more weeks, and everything would be fine. Julian snorted another line of cocaine. This being his second line in the past three hours, was more than he usually would take in 12 hours.

It gave him the capacity to think clearly. He would worry about cutting back his cocaine use once he achieved this next stage of his plan. He thought about how he would continue to finesse his addiction into a multibillion-dollar production. Although some said he relied purely on luck, his meticulous planning and years of experience made it possible for him to be so successful. He maintained one of the largest illegal drug manufacturing operations in North America. He supplied enormous markets now, such as New York City, Chicago, and Detroit, and made inroads into the Los Angeles and San Francisco markets.

His unique product created its own demand among those prone to develop addictions. The addition of remifentanil to cocaine caused the addiction to become overwhelmingly strong. The clients yearned for more of the same within a few hours. Profound addiction resulted from just one use. The drugs caused a powerful dopamine release, but because the remifentanil was a narcotic, there would be physical addiction. Narcotic withdrawal caused symptoms of tachycardia, sweating, anxiety, abdominal pains, cramps, nausea, and vomiting. This could only be relieved with more of this concoction.

Julian benefited from his time during medical school by studying with the neurophysiologist. He spent several summers working in his lab, researching. Julian compiled knowledge about addiction to drugs such as cocaine and remifentanil. He wrote papers on addiction and dopamine and gave talks at many addiction conferences. Although he now practiced as an orthopedic surgeon, he knew more about these drugs than anyone else. The reason remifentanil on its own was not the drug of choice for many opioid addicts was that it only has a very short half-life. The narcotic effect peaked in 4 minutes. With the combination of cocaine, the effect became so overwhelming that even after one use, the user would scramble to get more.

Julian had perfected the dosing requirements. They added just enough remifentanil in the cocaine mix to avoid respiratory depression and death. These highly addictive substances release large quantities of dopamine in the brain. Death from an overdose would be disastrous for business, so the dosing requirement must be accurate. They produced cocaine with 100% purity by not mixing it with other substances. He handed the distribution chain over to a network of distribution professionals. It astonished Julian how many people were involved in the drug distribution network. Many worked as professionals, such as doctors, nurses, bank managers, CEOs of large companies, and IT experts. Many became involved in managing their own addiction. Others became involved in financing their lavish lifestyle. The distributors of the illicit drug market refused to dilute the product. This might have the undesired effect of reducing the craving for more of the same product, and their clients might seek drugs elsewhere.

Julian started the business for three reasons. #1-To manage his cocaine addiction and have ready access to 100% pure cocaine. #2-To disappear once he could liquidate his assets and have enough money. #3-To completely change his identity so no one would ever find him. He would complete all his work during the last five years in less than two weeks. He just had to get through this latest setback involving Jeremy. It was time to place an important phone call.

"Hello, John? This is Julian Yacoby."

A moment of silence followed on the other end of the line. "Julian! I wasn't expecting to hear from you for two more weeks. How are things going?"

Julian quickly filled in the past few weeks' events with John

Papadopoulos. Julian met John three years ago while on holiday in Antigua, the West Indies. John, on his third rum punch at the bar of the Antigua Yacht Club, talked with Julian as he pulled up on a barstool beside him and ordered the same rum punch. After a few minutes of conversation, they discovered they were both sailors. Julian chartered a sailboat with a captain and crew to circumnavigate the island of Antigua, stopping at Barbuda along the way. The charter would take about a week. Julian met many interesting people along the way, including his newfound friend, John Papadopoulos.

John recounted his journey from his home in Greece and the move to Antigua to live on his 50-meter yacht. He explained he needed to escape the heavy taxes in Europe. Perhaps every 2 weeks, John would rent the massive yacht for $250,000/week. Running such a massive boat was expensive, costing perhaps $1.5 million annually. However, after paying all expenses, about $3 million a year tax-free continued to replenish his bank accounts year after year.

Julian recognized an edginess in John. An occasional repetitive knee movement while he was sitting on the barstool reflected an anxiety that was difficult to control. The uncertainty in John's eyes caused him to glance around the room at the slightest increase in noise as a startling effect. Repetitive nose wiping with a sleeve, as if to scratch an itch, contributed to the edginess. But the dilated pupils and bloodshot eyes gave away the cocaine habit.

In the bar's darkness, Julian leaned across and whispered into John's ear, "You look like you could use a line….."

That was the beginning of their 3-year friendship that turned into their successful business venture.

"I think we are going to have to move up our timetable," said Julian as he continued the conversation on the phone.

John said, "I have most of the pieces in place, but there are a few details I need to take care of. The purchase of the island in the Bahamas is almost complete. The $250 million bank draft needs to be wired to the escrow company, and I can do that in the next few days. This step will complete the transfer of ownership of the island to you. Getting the island registered in the name of the defunct cruise company you purchased proved difficult. I negotiated a high-level financial transaction with the minister of tourism. He seemed to settle down after we agreed upon a $10 million consultation fee for him. I took a circuitous pathway to make sure that your ownership remains untraceable. The last piece is the establishment of your new identity. I will keep you updated on that part once you leave Canada for good. It is paramount that none of the identity information gets out before then."

John had secretly acquired Julian's bank information, passwords, and bank accounts. He copied all this unbeknownst to Julian. During one of their previous meetings, he asked Julian to log into his bank account using John's laptop. John embedded a program to capture the keystrokes, web pages, bank account information and the 2-step verification codes. He would never access the drug dealer's information, which would be tantamount to a death sentence if caught. John was a believer that information is power. Sometimes perhaps in the future, when things get difficult, that power might come in useful.

Julian let out an immense sigh of relief. He developed a great deal of discomfort over the years, putting trust in others, especially when it involved cocaine users. He understood that the cocaine user will always put cocaine use ahead of any other obligation or promise made. The biggest risk when dealing with drug addicts involves trusting them. The best cocaine made on the market today came from Julian's production facility. He made certain of the 100% purity using industry-standard state-of-the-art technology. He never wavered in this principle of purity. This made it a lot easier to establish loyalty with cocaine addicts.

The phone call to John ended with the promise to stay in touch and talk in a few days to complete the plans.

Julian's dedicated cell phone to the drug production business rang, which startled Julian. Only a few trusted individuals accessed the number. The voice at the other end of the line said, "We have a problem."

Chapter 15

Jeremy woke up in pitch blackness. It totally disorientated him. He did not recall how he came to be where he discovered himself. The fogginess in his mind prevented him from thinking clearly. He lay in what looked like a 6 by 6-foot storage closet. Jeremy touched some cleaning supplies scattered on the floor and found what seemed to be a mop and bucket which rested next to him. He touched these things in the darkness with his hands, as there was no light coming into the room. His hands were bound with zip-lock ties. Slowly, his mind cleared. He remembered the drug manufacturing operation. Understanding how it connected to the church eluded his logically trained thinking process. The reverend's face flashed into his mind, but he did not understand the connection and why he found himself in this small room.

The zip-lock ties bound his hands tightly. The snugness of zip lock ties hindered the movement of his wrists, allowing only limited movement. He remembered something about a video on YouTube about how to free oneself from zip-lock ties. His mind, although still foggy, brought back the memory of watching the escape from zip ties. Jeremy recollected you must ensure the zip tie was tight and the connection clasp placed between the wrists. He grabbed the zip tie with his teeth and ensured it was as tight as it could be against his wrists. He recalled the next step. They forcefully brought their hands down against their tensed abdominal muscles. Jeremy raised his hands over his head and slammed both against the abdominal wall, resulting in a huge grunt, but the zip ties remained firmly in place. His hands got numb because the ties were too tight against his wrists. Jeremy held his hands above his head and gave it another try, but unfortunately, the same result occurred. Only this time, it drew the ties even tighter. His wrists became very numb now. A flash of anger passed through him, and a swear word escaped his lips. He lifted his hands high over his head and smashed them down forcibly against his abdominal muscles, which knocked him down onto the floor. However, the plastic snapped this time, and his hands were free. He massaged the wrists, and the numbness quickly abated.

While thinking about his next move, he heard footsteps outside the storage closet. Still somewhat confused about where he was and how he got there, Jeremy pretended to still be unconscious. He grabbed the cloth end of the mop to use as a weapon if necessary. The door opened, and light flooded into the room. From the corner of his eye, he saw two men in hazmat suits. They looked down at him.

"It looks like he is still unconscious," said one of them. Julian recognized that voice. The reverend's distinctive Irish brogue accent boomed through. "I gave him enough ketamine to knock out a horse. We'll keep him locked up in here 'til we figure out our next steps."

They turned around to leave. With catlike speed, Jeremy jumped to his feet and jammed the end of the mop into the abdomen of the first of the men. Jeremy impaled the end of the mop handle upwards to the left side of the abdomen. The forward motion of the handle seemed to stop when it pushed against the diaphragm. There was a whooshing sound as it knocked the wind out of him. He crumpled in the doorway and moaned, holding his abdomen. Jeremy capitalized on the first swing, twirling the mop around and hitting the second man in the face with the wooden part of the handle. A massive gush of blood from his nose followed the resulting crunching sound. The hands of the second man involuntarily flew to his face as if to protect himself from another blow. Instead, Jeremy took the end of the mop handle and rammed it into his soft abdomen. He aimed the trajectory upwards to cause as much damage as possible to the internal organs. The second man fell to the floor. The hands moved down to protect his abdomen. With the end of the mop as a battering ram, Jeremy smashed it into his unprotected face until he stopped all movement.

Jeremy then turned towards the first man, likely the reverend, who now lay facedown, still moaning while clutching his belly. He swung the handle against the back of the head. He stopped moving. Holding the mop like a baseball bat, Jeremy's eyes flickered back and forth between the two men. He detected no movement from either of them. By this time, Jeremy was panting.

The adrenaline coursing through his body forced him to be wide awake. He needed to get out of there in a hurry.

Jeremy recognized his surroundings as the church's basement. The many receptions held down there following the special events, such as confirmations or baptisms, flashed through his mind. The stairs led directly to the front of the church. He opened the door and ran down the stairs to the sidewalk. Still dressed in his running attire, he picked up the pace and headed home. In his mind, Jeremy constructed a plan while he ran. The initial step he came up with was to call his lawyer, Michael, for counsel. Jeremy's recommendation would be to contact the police to raid the drug production facility. It was difficult for Jeremy to comprehend how this was happening right under their noses. Within 20 minutes at a fast pace, he arrived breathless at home and walked through the front door. Iona usually worked from home, but Jeremy did not see her through the glass door of her office.

His cell phone rang. He did not recognize the number, so he let it go to voicemail. The same number rang again, and he let it go to voicemail. When the phone rang a third time, he answered it. "Listen to me carefully," said the voice.

"Who the hell is this?" asked Jeremy.

"We have Iona. Follow our instructions precisely or risk her being harmed. Do you understand?"

"If you touch one hair on her body, I will hunt and kill you. Do you understand that?" screamed Jeremy. "I am going to hang up and call the police. Do you understand that?"

A bloodcurdling scream resonated through the phone. "No, no, don't, please, no!" Jeremy could hear the desperation and panic in Iona's voice as she pleaded not to be hurt.

Jeremy felt faint. Speaking was no longer possible for him. He sat on the wooden floor and held his head in his hands so he wouldn't faint. He wept. This could not be happening. He could not control his sobbing. "Don't hurt her," Jeremy whispered into the phone. "I'll do anything."

"That's more like it," said the voice at the other end. Jeremy could hear Iona softly crying in the background.

"#1- You must not call the police. #2-You must not speak to anyone about this or what you saw underneath the church. #3-You must answer your cell phone when I call. I will call again in 24 hours. Iona's life depends on you following these three simple instructions." The phone became dead as the voice disconnected from the call.

Jeremy lay down on the sofa, defeated. The adrenaline rush he experienced earlier when he battered his captors with the mop handle disappeared as quickly as it came. A sense of dread and fear permeated through his body. He couldn't think. He needed Iona to guide him about what to do next. The television was on. The news droned as a dull buzzing sound. He suddenly felt exhausted. He tried to fight to fall asleep. There was so much that he needed to sort out. The effects of the ketamine had not totally escaped from his body, and before he could prevent it, he slipped into a dreamless black hole.

Sometime later, Jeremy woke up. He immediately remembered that Iona was gone, kidnapped by evil and corrupt men, and it was all his fault. The TV was blaring. A news item got his attention. The police announced to be on the lookout for the person who mercilessly assaulted a reverend and his co-worker in the church next to the hospital. Both men were undergoing surgery at the Metropolitan Hospital. They described their injuries as extensive. Their conditions were critical. The police had no further information, such as why an attack occurred or who might be responsible.

Someone was knocking at his door. Jeremy slowly got up from the sofa so as not to fall. He felt faint. He made his way to the door and opened it. It was Julian.

"Is everything OK?" said Julian. "I thought I would just drop by and check on you."

"This is truly a surprise," said Jeremy, trying to control his voice so that he would seem to talk normally. "Things are fine. I would ask you to come inside, but I'm under the weather."

"Let me know if there's anything I can do," said Julian. "I'll let you get some rest, and we will talk soon. Don't be a stranger. I'm here to help."

Jeremy had a tingling sensation going up his neck as he walked away. Something about Julian convinced him that the reason for his visit did not match what he said. All his senses told him that Julian was insincere. Jeremy could not place his finger on it precisely. As he stood in the doorway, Julian suspiciously looked over Jeremy's shoulder, inspecting the front hallway. Perhaps looking for something or someone? Julian's eyes were darting around as if anxious. The slight blood tinge to the whites of his eyes suggested there was more to Julian's visit other than the concern for his well-being.

Jeremy paced back and forth in the living room of his house. He needed to understand what was going on. He wanted to better understand cocaine addiction and drug production operations. The only person he trusted was his close friend, Dr. Rick Mandel. Rick and Jeremy journeyed through medical school together. Although they completed their residency at the same institution, they trained in different fields. Jeremy trained through the surgery program, and Rick trained in psychiatry. Rick became the addiction specialist at the hospital. His interest in neurophysiology made Rick more knowledgeable about addiction than anyone else Jeremy ever met.

"Hello Rick, this is Jeremy."

"Jeremy, my good friend, I've been waiting for your call. I didn't want to interfere with your troubles, but I am so glad you have finally called."

"Rick, I'm in a spot of trouble, as you must have heard from the hospital scuttlebutt. Can you drop by the house? We need to talk. I'm unsure if anyone is watching the house, so could you come around the back door? I don't want to be too cloak and dagger, but strange things are happening."

"See you in about 15 minutes. I'll park two blocks away and will come through the back alley. I'll knock on your back door. I will ensure that no one sees me and that I am not followed."

Jeremy let Rick in through the back door when he arrived exactly 15 minutes after the phone call. They hugged each other and patted each other on the back.

"Let's go into the study," said Jeremy.

They sat down, and Jeremy recounted the entire series of events over the past week. It took about an hour. Although Jeremy took a risk telling Rick everything, he needed to clear his mind and share his grief with someone he trusted. He trusted Rick completely. Jeremy showed the videos. He shared his suspicion that someone snuck into the room immediately before Charlene Simpson's death.

He showed the Excel spreadsheet that Iona and he started and how the arrows connected some events. Finally, Jeremy revealed to Rick that someone had kidnapped Iona.

"All of those events are all connected," said Rick.

"What I really need from you, Rick is some background information about drug addiction. I need to know how it affects behavior so I understand what I'm up against here. All the arrows on my wall are pointing back to drugs." Said Jeremy.

"We've been friends for a long time, Jeremy, and it sounds like you're in a heap of trouble through no fault of your own. We haven't discussed our professional developments over the past few years, so I will fill you in.

"I have a PhD in neurophysiology. I largely focused my psychiatric practice on drug addiction. We link the shared pathway to addiction to a deficit of dopamine receptors in the brain. We all need dopamine just to feel normal and to function normally. In the last two years, the number of patients addicted to cocaine has skyrocketed. Most people may not be aware of the fact that about 10% of the population has a predisposition to addiction. In our city, for example, we're talking about half a million people that can develop an addiction. Brain damage can reduce dopamine receptors caused by traumatic events, such as seen with PTSD. Other patients appear to have a genetic fault, leading to fewer dopamine sites in the brain. Whatever the cause, the effect is the same. These individuals need that extra jolt of dopamine release just to function. It's poorly understood, but some people get that extra dopamine release by smoking cigarettes; others get the same release by gambling; others get this from alcohol; and the most severe addictions require cocaine and opioids.

"Julian Yacoby worked in my lab as a medical student. He has learned more about these drugs than anyone else. I'm 100% certain he's a cocaine addict. He is extremely intelligent. I would peg his IQ at around 160. He is also a psychopath, shown by his charm and manipulation. He meets all the DSM-5 TR criteria for a psychopath. I occasionally encounter a patient with this mix of intelligence, addiction, and psychopathic traits. It is the most dangerous combination for a psychiatrist to deal with. I have met no one so dangerous as Julian."

Jeremy sat there in complete silence, taking in every word Rick said. As so many times in the past, his 6th sense about people remained intact, correctly pegging Julian as something other than he seems what Rick said to fit in perfectly with his observations about Julian. "What does DSM-5 TR stand for?"

"That's the psychiatric bible for diagnosing mental health disorders. It stands for Diagnostic and Statistical Manual of Mental Disorders. The 5 TR part is the most up-to-date version," said Rick.

"Something else you should understand about cocaine addicts," said Rick. "For them, it's all about cocaine. It is as if they erased all other moral codes from their souls. Once down that path, it is nothing for them to steal, lie, cheat, and commit other horrendous crimes, even murder. They will go to any lengths to keep the flow of cocaine through their system. The drug addiction scene has been intense lately because they added something else to the cocaine that magnifies the addiction. I suspect it is a narcotic that is added in the perfect dosage. It will not cause respiratory depression and death, but there is enough to magnify the craving, so they will do anything for the next hit."

Jeremy said, "Wow! Those are some powerful allegations that you are firing at me. Can you explain how everything fits in? What caused my patient's death? How can the hospital support someone like Julian and make him chief of surgery? How do you explain the medical advisory committee not supporting me?"

"I do not possess the answer to those questions. Given the support that the medical advisory committee showed for Julian, I suspect that the answer to all those questions rests with activities involving Julian," said Rick. "There is something else I want you to look at."

Rick pulled up in front of Jeremy's computer and logged onto the hospital foundation website. "The Department of

Psychiatry recently received a huge grant from the foundation. They donated about $10 million to upgrade the department and to conduct research. When I checked where this came from, there appeared to be an anonymous donation about six months ago for $10 million." Rick used the cursor to highlight the donation. "I then searched 'anonymous donations. It turns out that the hospital has received about $50 million over the past two years. I then checked other hospitals around the city. The largest anonymous donation I found was $50,000, but most were less than $10,000. You must ask what is going on with these anonymous donations?"

Jeremy 's eyes widen, this being the first time he heard about any of these donations. He donated over $50,000 to the hospital over the past 10 years, but the hospital always asked for more donations. The hospital board instructed him in his role as chief of surgery to look for potential donors and speak with them. He thought he developed a great relationship with the foundation board through the hard work he shared with them. The surprise anonymous donations completely caught him off guard. The board should have shared and celebrated these amounts of money with the hospital staff.

"A few final thoughts," said Rick. "My advice to you is to assume that Julian is behind everything that happened. Genetics gifted him with high intelligence. His abhorrent childhood likely caused his lack of empathy and lack of introspection. But the most powerful driving force for him is his cocaine addiction. Although the connections between all the events are not obvious now, they will all point to Julian at some point. Of that, I am certain."

"So, you say that Julian is responsible for taking Iona?" said Jeremy.

"For someone like Julian, it is all about control. He has been observing you for years. I suspect he concluded that the best way to control you is through Iona. Although he may have no capacity for empathy, he can manipulate this. He may not understand your feelings towards Iona, but he acknowledges they exist. Using your love for her to his advantage is not a problem for him. You will probably do as instructed to protect Iona from harm, which will keep you quiet about what you saw."

"I was told not to speak with anyone," said Jeremy. "But I am glad I spoke with you, as I think I better understand what I am up against. One advantage I have is that if what you say is correct about Julian, he believes he is smarter than anybody else. Clearly, he is not as smart as he thinks he is. You have him figured out. He will soon find out that he is not smarter than me!"

Chapter 16

Jeremy was restless. He still paced the floor, desperately trying to devise a plan. It was 1:00 o'clock in the morning. Rick left out the back door about an hour before. Trying to sleep was a waste of time. Being far too wound up, he put on his running gear with his shorts and singlet and a headlamp, which he kept turned off for the time being. He headed towards the church but doubled back a few times to ensure no one followed or watched him. He wanted a better look at the drug production facility. He betted that with the reverend in the hospital with at least one of his co-workers, this would be the last thing anyone would expect him to do. The run took 20 minutes.

He hid in the shrubs at the rear. The full moon lit up the garden behind the church. They turned the lights off. Jeremy detected no human activity in or around the premises. No burglar alarms protected the church. Reverend Rowen always told him during his visits to his office over the years that they would welcome anyone and everyone, day or night. Jeremy didn't have a plan, so he stayed hidden for about 10 minutes to confirm the absence of activity. There had to be another entrance. The church was right next door to the hospital, and if there were an entrance, that's where it would be. Jeremy had no access to the hospital because the security team confiscated his hospital access card. Detection would be a certainty should he attempt to enter the hospital because there were over 1600 cameras. The videos would capture his every move. He had no good reason to be in the hospital since he was on a voluntary leave of absence. He would have to risk going into the church like last time.

Jeremy made his way to the front door, trying to stay in the shadows of the garden on the way in case someone guarded the entrance to the church. He looked around again and saw no one. The locked doors prevented him from opening them. He made his way around the side of the church and climbed up, and looked through the window, using the trellis against the stone wall. He recognized this as the same room where he had left his cell phone. Jeremy climbed down the trellis and looked for a tool he could use to break the window. A small tool shed stood at the back of the garden. He easily broke the lock and chose a hammer. He saw other tools, such as rakes and shovels, but he thought they might be too cumbersome. The hammer would also double as a weapon if he encountered anyone.

He climbed up the trellis to the window and broke a part of the window. Jeremy put his hand inside to release the latch to open the window. He scraped the broken glass from the ledge so he would not cut himself and crawled inside. It was dark, but a small amount of light shone through the window from the full moon. He tried to open the door that would lead down the stairway. The locked door prevented him from entering. Using the hammer, he pried the door open. He looked around the hallway for cameras and motion detectors, and there did not appear to be anything that would record his activity. No light entered the hallway, so pitch blackness surrounded Jeremy. To see better, he turned on his headlight. He made his way down the stairs and along the long hallway. A locked door prevented his entry when he got to the end. He easily opened it with his hammer. Slowly, Jeremy opened the door and expected to see a lot of activity. Instead of bright lights, only pitch blackness remained. The room was totally empty of any equipment and furniture. Gone were the large vats at the end of the room. Gone were the fume cupboards, the tables, and any evidence of a production facility there. Jeremy looked around incredulously. This happened in less than 12 hours.

Using his headlight, he walked around the room. He noticed a pneumatic tube system like the one in the hospital in one corner of the space. The instructions on the side explained how to send the pneumatic tube to different areas of the medical facility. A large garage door appeared when he reached the end of the room. The locked door prevented him from seeing what was on the other side. Despite using the hammer, he could not open it. He thought he should probably leave, as sticking around would gain nothing. He left the same way he came in.

Jeremy made his way back to the house. He entered through the back door to avoid any suspicion that someone was watching him. After everything that had happened that day, it completely overwhelmed him with exhaustion. He lay down on his bed and, within seconds, passed out into a fitful sleep.

Jeremy awoke to the sound of his cell phone. He instantly sat up in his bed and answered the call. The same voice spoke. "I trust you have been following my last set of instructions. I want you to listen carefully. Iona's life depends on it. This morning, head to your sailboat and head out on Lake Ontario. You will speak with no one. You will sail across Lake Ontario to Oswega, New York. The Marina at Oswega will take off your mast and help you load it onto the deck of your boat. You will then traverse the locks through the Erie Canal. Riverside Marina will rig your mast using their crane. You will then motor down the Hudson River to New York City. You will receive further instructions then. I will follow you on the sailboat tracker, so do not deviate from this route." The phone went dead.

"Wait. Wait. I need confirmation that Iona is OK!" screamed Jeremy in the dial tone. He sat down. He thought about his options. They would know if he didn't leave on his sailboat because his tracker sent GPS signals every 15 minutes. This kind of trip should take weeks of planning. Normally, wise sailors only attempted to cross the lake when the weather was optimal. The fuel tanks needed to be filled with diesel. Enough food and water for a week would need to be stocked. A crew is necessary to help navigate the lock system to hold the boat in place while the locks fill up. The extra crew prevented the turbulence from smashing the boat against the walls.

To organize his erratic thoughts, he created a list. His Transport Canada papers and passport were necessary for the boat. He would bring his US cruising permit. With his Nexus card, Immigration and Customs on the US side were a breeze. He filled up a cooler full of frozen food from the freezer, some bread, pasta, rice, spaghetti sauce, and cold cuts and emptied the fridge. He had about $1000 in US currency for supplies to be purchased along the Hudson River if needed.

Jeremy loaded all the supplies into his car and headed towards the Yacht Club. After parking his car, he loaded the supplies into a cart and brought them to the sailboat. He purchased his 51-foot sailboat, a Hanse 508, only two years ago. He bought the sailboat as part of his retirement plan, which he hoped to enact in about seven or eight years. He loved his sailboat, and with Iona's agreement, they named her Sailing Vessel *Iona*. He decided to learn how to sail the boat in the shelter of Lake Ontario before setting sail into the open expanse of the Caribbean, which he had dreamed of since he was little. Jeremy was still mastering the art of sailing the boat and had never done a voyage alone. On race nights, he would have a crew of about six or seven experienced sailors to assist him. He hoped to call on some of them to help him take the boat across the lake, but the instructions were clear. He must do it by himself.

Chapter 17

A blustery wind gusted from the northeast at around 35 knots. The icy wind blasted across the marina, where *Iona* rocked gently in the protected harbor. The Coast Guard issued a small craft warning, advising all boats to stay off the lake. Despite the warning, Jeremy cast off and headed into the rough waters of Lake Ontario. Jeremy donned his foul weather gear, but the stiff wind found its way into the clothing, causing him to shiver. With his winter gloves and hat covering his head and hands, his eyes were the only part exposed to the weather. He placed three reefs in the mainsail to reduce the wind pressure. The small jib sail was partially furled to reduce exposure to the strong wind. The enormous waves caused the sailboat to bounce around with such force preventing Jeremy from moving safely around the deck. Every wave would come crashing into the dodger, the canvas protecting the front of the cockpit, which took the brunt of the force. The dodger prevented most of the water from entering the cockpit, but every third wave would crash into Jeremy. Some of the cold water would force its way through the small gap that allowed his eyes to see out of the foul weather gear and percolate down to his boots. He rapidly became sopping wet and miserable. In better conditions, the autopilot assisted with maneuvering the boat. Because of the rough seas, the autopilot stopped working, and he had to steer the boat by hand.

He battled the elements on the lake for about 6 hours. He realized it would take at least another 12 hours to get to Oswega. Jeremy had an intense urge to urinate but could not leave the helm for a few seconds as the boat would careen out of control. He remembered reading in one of his many sailing magazines about a maneuver called "heaving to". Although he had never tried it, he read the concept was to enable the jib to be on one side of the breeze and the mainsail to be on the other. "Heaving to" keep the bow of the boat into the wind. This stopped the boat's progress and made it possible for it to rock calmly with the seas.

He fixed the jib in place and steered the boat into the wind so that the mainsail was now on the other side of the wind. The swaying of the boat right away changed into a very smooth movement. The winds and the force of the waves against the boat settled. The boat's speed fell to zero. Jeremy set the auto helm so that the rudder would not move. After he was confident it was safe to do so, he descended below to the toilet. He removed all his wet clothes and dried himself. The closest shore, about 10 miles away, reduced the danger he would run aground. For the first time on the trip, he was safe. He crawled into the forward bunk and fell asleep for a one-hour power nap.

He woke up after two hours. The gentle motion of the boat caused him to sleep longer than he had initially planned. He hoped that the delay would not be a problem for Iona. That was all he thought about. Considering his options, the only option available involved following the instructions that the voice on the telephone demanded. Jeremy deduced the only chance he had to see Iona again meant he must follow the cryptic instructions. He recognized that although it was a slim chance, it was the only chance. He resolved he would not jeopardize that one chance.

The digital time read 7 pm on the chart plotter. It also told him the trip to Oswega, New York, would take another twelve hours. In the two hours following his nap, the wind settled. It now blew 25 knots, allowing the sailing to be comfortable. Sailing in 25 knots of wind frequently occurred on race nights at the sailing club during the summer. He donned his wet foul weather gear. Although the clothes were damp, he ascended the companionway stairs into the cockpit. The rain fortunately stopped. The size of the waves had settled. He trimmed the jib and mainsail so the sails swung around to work together on the same wind side. The boat responded like a thoroughbred horse and took off. The motion on the deck became gentler than before, and he no longer got soaked by the waves. It would be a long night, but he was confident he could manage.

As the night wore on, the conditions settled even further. He used the auto helm to steer the boat. They equipped the boat with Starlink internet, allowing him to fill out the arrival information on the ROAM app. for US customs and immigration. The question stumped him. "What is the purpose of your visit?" Because he did not know the answer to this, Jeremy wrote optimistically, "I'm meeting my wife in New York for the weekend, and we will stay on the sailboat."

Within a few minutes, the app. responded, "We approve your stay."

He arrived in Oswega, New York, around 7:30 AM. None of the staff arrived at the dockyard for such an early hour. Jeremy tied the sailboat up in front of the mast crane of Oswega Marina. The wind settled completely. The calm waters in the protected harbor allowed him to tie up to the dock lines unassisted. Jeremy appreciated perhaps he was a better sailor than he gave himself credit. He disassembled all the rigging and removed the sails himself. Using sail ties, he removed the canvas from the dodger and bimini, bundling them up. To store them in the sail locker, he took them to the front of the boat. Jeremy opened the latch to the sail locker and was about to throw in the canvas when he stopped. The sail locker was completely full. They packed it to the ceiling with bags and bags of white powder covered in plastic.

"Those pricks!" the words escaped from Jeremy's lips.

"Need a hand with anything?" asked a voice from the pier.

With the hatch to the sail locker open, Jeremy worried that the man offering help would see the stash of drugs. The opened lid of the hatch blocked the view of the person asking the question.

Jeremy slammed the lid closed before the man could see the contents. "My crew must have filled up the sail locker with all kinds of junk, so there is no room for this canvas. No worries, I'll put them down below. I'm Jeremy" He held out his hand.

"Oscar. Pleased to meet you." As he shook hands with Jeremy. "I'm the harbor master, crane operator, cook and chief bottle washer. There will just be the two of us taking off your mast. Can you manage?"

"I'm sure that we'll do just fine."

Taking off the mast using the crane took about two hours. They situated the mast on some wooden struts. They wrapped the lines around the mast and removed the spreaders. The next step involved constructing the cradle so the mast rested on the sailboat's deck. This took another two hours. They put the mast on top of the cradles and fastened it. The mast hung over the stern and the boat's bow by about 8 feet. "That should get you under the bridges of the canal, no problem," said Oscar.

"Are you apprehensive about navigating the lock system alone?" asked Oscar. "The turbulence created when they let the water in can really throw a boat around, even one your size."

"I have never done this, so I'm not sure what to expect from the locks," said Jeremy.

"If you like, I could ask my cousin Ralph to guide you through the locks. You would have to pay for his bus trip from Albany to Oswega, but he could use the extra cash. You should pay him about $100 a day and include food. It will probably take three days to get to Albany."

Jeremy thought about this for a minute. His biggest concern was that this Ralph person might discover the hidden cocaine. Jeremy realized he could prevent accidental discovery by putting the heavy sails on top of the hatch to the sail locker. There would be no way to get into the sail locker without much effort to move the sails. The sails would need to be attached to a halyard to lift them off the sail locker. The only way to lift the sails would be to use the electric winch. This would not be possible until they put up the mast in Albany.

"Ralph sounds like a great addition. Can we leave in an hour? I'd like to get a move on," said Jeremy. "How much do I owe you?"

"It was pre-paid, so nothing more. I'll give Ralph a call now." Oscar said as he pulled out his cell phone.

The knowledge that someone had paid for the work beforehand shocked Jeremy. Tracking the sailboat did not bother Jeremy as it was easy to track any sailing vessel these days using the internet. AIS (Automatic identification system) technology allowed anyone worldwide to follow his sailboat. Modern marine radios equipped each vessel with a radio signal that emitted a frequency specific to that boat. This signal broadcasted to satellites that picked up the frequency every 15 minutes. AIS was installed on most seagoing vessels. Jeremy would work out a plan to mess up the drug organization that held his wife captive while sailing down the Hudson River, despite his being tracked. He had plenty of time to come up with a solid plan.

Chapter 18

Jeremy became tired as he approached New York City on his sailboat from the Hudson River. The trip until this point had been relatively uneventful as he reflected on the journey from Oswega. Replacing the mast on the top of the deck in Albany proceeded smoothly. He rigged the rest of the boat and put the jib on the bow of the boat and the mainsail on the boom. *Iona* was ready to sail when necessary. The crane operator at Riverside Marina helped Jeremy put the boat back together. Jeremy and Ralph successfully negotiated the 30 locks of the Erie Canal System. Ralph, clearly experienced in moving boats safely through the locks, had done this before. Placing the fenders alongside the hull as the boat rested against the concrete walls of the locks prevented damage as the locks filled or emptied. He would fix the rope in the midship to keep the boat parallel to the wall. This allowed the flooding water of the lock system to nuzzle the boat upwards gently without damage.

The locks closed for the evening at 5:00 PM and opened the following morning at 7:00 AM. Jeremy was the first in the lock system every morning when it opened. It took two full days to traverse the 30 locks before he arrived in Albany. He would have described the landscape along for Hudson River under better circumstances as spectacular. Jeremy, however, had so many other thoughts on his mind that he could not enjoy the beauty. He remained worried sick about Iona, who never left his thoughts. At night, he kept motoring, hoping to get to New York City faster. That way, he would get to Iona faster and help her to safety. Jeremy remained awake without sleep for the past two days.

The cell phone rang, which jolted Jeremy out of his dark thoughts. "Keep heading out to sea through New York City," said the voice on the phone. "Head for this waypoint. N22.30 W72.33. It will take you about five days to get there." The phone signal died.

Jeremy suddenly became totally alert. "Wait. Wait," he yelled into the phone, "I have to speak to Iona. I need to find out if she is OK." Jeremy spoke into a disconnected line. When he punched the redial button, the digital message appeared "This number is no longer in service." A sense of helplessness filled his every thought. He entered the waypoint that the voice gave him into his chart plotter. This made it certain that he did not forget the coordinates. He steered the boat into the New York harbor, past the Statue of Liberty and into the open ocean.

Jeremy, dead tired after no sleep for the last 48 hours, had trouble keeping his eyes open. Sleep deprivation was a frequent occurrence after working as a surgeon for all those years. He taught himself to perfect techniques to keep awake at the most crucial times. However, he had exhausted his repertoire. A plan developed despite the lack of sleep and the ability to think clearly. He set the radar and the AIS to alarm if a vessel got within one nautical mile of his boat. That way, he slept a few hours without worrying about a collision with another vessel. When he left New York harbor, he navigated the boat south towards the waypoint he entered in the chart plotter. That waypoint was 200 nautical miles off San Sebastian Island in the Bahama. As he recalled, this marked the first point of land that Christopher Columbus reached after his epic voyage across the Atlantic. The wind blew at 25 knots from the northeast. He set the sails, and as he ran with the wind, the boat's motion became gentle, and the waves traveled in the same direction as the boat. Jeremy set the auto helm to aim for the waypoint, set the alarms, and curled up in the cockpit. Within 30 seconds, he fell into a deep sleep.

Chapter 19

"Sailing vessel Iona, sailing vessel Iona, sailing vessel Iona, this is the freighter, Magnolia," blasted the VHF handheld radio on the cockpit table.

Jeremy woke up confused. Pitch blackness prevented him from understanding his whereabouts. Half asleep, he mumbled something to the radio to the effect that Iona was not here and that he was searching for her, too. It took about 3 seconds for him to realize he was on the water and getting hailed on his VHF radio. He reached over to the cockpit table, grabbed the radio, and pressed the transmit button as he spoke. "Freighter Magnolia, freighter Magnolia, freighter Magnolia, this is sailing vessel, Iona."

"Iona, let's go to channel 69."

Jeremy adjusted the VHF radio to channel 69 and said, "Magnolia, this is Iona".

"Hi, Iona; I just wanted to ensure you could see us. We are about half a nautical mile dead ahead of you. I wanted to let you know we adjusted our course about 10 degrees away from your port side. I hope you can adjust 10 degrees to your starboard, and we will pass by a safe margin."

"Roger that, Magnolia. 10 degrees to my starboard. This is Iona, over and out," said Jeremy.

Jeremy adjusted the course heading and then adjusted the sails. He slept for over 4 hours. Still, sleep deprived, his mind and his body were functioning at a level that would be safe. Reviewing the course on the chart plotter, he realized he would reach that waypoint in about 5 days. That timing assumed he maintained his speed of nine knots. In the middle of the ocean, hundreds of miles from the nearest shore, the waypoint ensured no other boat traffic. Jeremy accepted another boat would meet him before he reached that waypoint. Before they caught up with him, he had to come up with a solid plan. He presumed they would kill or push him overboard once they transferred the drugs. He had 5 days to come up with an ironclad plan. For now, he needed to look at the weather.

Jeremy downloaded the most recent weather forecast to his laptop using his PredictWind app. A few concerning features appeared on the weather map. The wind came from the northeast. He would cross the Gulf Stream in about 24 hours. The wind blew into the Gulf Stream against the current of 4-5 knots. He read that this might cause huge standing waves that damaged even the best-designed sailboats. The weather predicted the winds would get stronger over the next 36 hours. Once past the Gulf Stream, that same northeast wind would help him gain miles toward his destination and to his wife, Iona. The other option was to avoid the inclement weather. He could turn the boat around and head north until the low-pressure system passed. This would cause a 48 to 72-

hour delay. Any delay caused anxiety for Jeremy. He took the chance that the gigantic waves would not cause his 51-foot ocean-going sailboat to capsize. Although new to ocean sailing, he would soon find out if his *Iona* would rise to the challenge.

The wind continued to build from the northeast over the next 12 hours. Jeremy looked at the map of the Gulf Stream and adjusted his course so that he would cross at the narrowest part, about 45 miles across. At that point, the current took a slight bend towards the southeast. This put the wind on the beam, so the NE wind was positioned at right angles to the Gulf Stream current. Jeremy calculated this might be the best place to cross and to experience the fewest gigantic waves with the least chance of capsizing. He would cross this point in about 12 hours, so he planned to catch up on some sleep. He slept in the cockpit, ready to spring into action at a moment's notice.

Jeremy needed to feed himself, as a rough crossing may prevent him from preparing food. Jeremy set the alarms. It was unlikely he would encounter any other boats in this area of the North Atlantic, hundreds of miles from the shipping lanes. The warnings posted on the Internet about this low-pressure system caused Jeremy concern. The coastguard advised all boats to avoid this region of the ocean. For safety, Jeremy shortened his mainsail to the third reef and furled the jib, which was now about 1/2 the size. The reduction in sail surface did not make any difference to the boat's speed as *Iona* sliced through the rough waters effortlessly.

The sudden dumping of Jeremy on the cockpit floor by an enormous wave woke him up. He wore his life jacket, as always, when he sailed. Jeremy tied himself into the cockpit with a tether. To keep himself safe in rough seas, he secured jack lines and tied himself to the boat. He strategically placed the jack lines along the cockpit and the sailboat's deck. He moved anywhere safely, always tied to the boat with his tether. The pitching of the boat became erratic. The boat bounced from left to right as it fell off the steep cliffs that spewed vast quantities of seawater into the boat. Water filled the cockpit when a wave surged over the vessel's side. Jeremy risked getting catapulted into the water. The only thing that prevented getting washed over the side into the ocean was the tether that kept him lashed in. He had entered the Gulf Stream.

Things seemed to get worse over the next 30 minutes. The auto helm could no longer manage the gigantic waves and once again packed it in, refusing to steer the boat when the waves were so forceful. Jeremy grabbed the steering wheel before the boat rounded up into the wind. This would have been dangerous with these enormous waves and the size and shape of elephants. Jeremy steered the boat so that she slid down the waves. This prevented the waves from crashing into the cockpit. As he traveled deeper into the Gulfstream, the waves became wilder. It became difficult to predict whether he was going to slide down the wave or whether the wave would come crashing into the side of the boat. The night being pitch black alerted all his other senses. He listened to the roar of the ocean as a wave approached.

Jeremy hung onto the steering wheel tightly when the boat suddenly fell over on its side. He floated in the water after he lost his grip on the steering wheel. At first, he thought he floated underneath the boat. He held his breath, which seemed to last forever. How much longer he could hold his breath created a sense of panic. He remained under the water, and it seemed to boil around him. Suddenly, he experienced a sharp tug on his tether and witnessed all the water drain out of the cockpit through the back of the boat. The only thing that kept him attached to the boat was the tether.

Uncertain about what had happened, Jeremy thought the sailboat turned upside down, so-called "turtling". He saw the mast remained in place, as was the boom. He understood that if a sailboat "turtled", the heavy keel would help the boat come upright, but in doing so, the force of the water would break the mast in half. Instead, the wall of water from the breaking wave forced the sails flat against the ocean. The keel had righted the boat with no harm to the rigging. They commonly described this event as a "knockdown". When Jeremy thought he was upside down, likely a rogue wave smashed into the side of the boat, and the turbulence disorientated him. He breathed a sigh of relief. Jeremy felt lucky to be alive.

When he checked the chart plotter, he had successfully traversed the Gulf Stream. The warm air temperature starkly contrasted with the cold of the North Atlantic just 45 miles to the north. He checked the instruments for the temperature of the water, and it read 28 degrees Celsius. Wind velocity stabilized at 20 knots, and the sea became calmer. The auto helm managed the seas. Experiencing the knockdown emotionally depleted his resilience after the knockdown. The near-death experience caused intense fatigue. He lay down in the cockpit in his wet clothes and passed out.

Chapter 20

When Jeremy awoke, calmness dominated the seas. The sun shone with the storm having passed through the night. Jeremy walked around the boat's deck, using the jack lines and tether as a safety. He determined that there was minor damage to the rigging. *Iona* met the challenge of the storm and survived. He looked at the charts and saw that he still needed 3 1/2 days to reach his waypoint. He needed to devise a plan to save Iona and himself from certain death after the drug transfer to the dealers.

It came to him after about 20 minutes of deep thought. He purchased a remote starter for his BBQ last summer. Jeremy strapped the barbeque onto the railing at the stern of the boat. Sometimes a strong wind made the barbeque difficult to light. By opening the lid to start the barbeque, the wind often blew out the flame. He solved the problem by using a remote BBQ starter.

He needed leverage to get Iona and himself to safety. His plan involved covering the cocaine bags with gasoline-soaked rags. He buried the barbeque in the pile of cocaine in the sail locker. With the hatch to the sail locker tightly closed, the explosion would blow up the boat with the cocaine to dust. Jeremy envisioned the threat of blowing up the boat and their valuable cocaine would be enough for the kidnappers to do what he said. He wanted Iona to be safe with him as he imagined the two of them racing towards the horizon in the inflatable dinghy. He imagined having his finger on the controls using the Starlink internet system to trigger the remote.

Jeremy spent the next 2 days reviewing the plan and, in his mind, played out the various scenarios. The captors would likely come to him by speedboat. They would likely bring Iona in case they needed to leverage anything from him. There would be more than one person on board. It would happen during the daytime, as nighttime posed difficulties because of darkness on the open ocean. Jeremy suspected they would have weapons. He expected they would end up trying to kill both him and Iona. Jeremy also banked on the principle that cocaine was the only thing important to these people. He convinced himself that their fear of having the cocaine blown to dust would make them easier to manipulate. The more he thought about the plan, the more comfortable he became. He was entering with a strong negotiating position.

The boat sailed herself as the trade winds filled in from the east. The seas were gentle as the wind shaped the sails with the warm breeze and pulled *Iona* through the ocean at 9 knots. Jeremy filled his time by revisiting his plan from all angles. He imagined how the conversation would go. He followed the different paths where the discussion might head. Jeremy tried to get as much rest as possible. He ensured he was well hydrated and fed, as he would likely need all his strength.

The phone rang. Before the voice at the other end could begin, Jeremy spoke. "I'm going to do the talking," said Jeremy. "You should understand that I rigged the boat, so it will explode if you do not follow my instructions. Just so you know, I installed a remote starter for my BBQ and buried it in the cocaine. I have the cocaine covered in gasoline-soaked rags, and I will blow this boat to Kingdom come if you do not do what I say. All I want is Iona. I need to know that she is safe."

"She's safe. I'll let you speak with her," said the voice at the other end.

There was silence at the other end for about 30 seconds. "Jeremy," said Iona. "I'm OK"

Iona was never one to dramatize any situation. She was always the calming influence of the two. When Jeremy sometimes lost his temper, Iona brought him back to earth, allowing him to think rationally. She analyzed any situation and developed well-thought-out and practical solutions. Jeremy believed that if Iona knew about his plan to blow up the boat, she would try to talk him out of it and into a more sensible plan.

"Honey, you do not know how good it is to hear your voice," Jeremy suddenly choked up, and although he tried to speak, no words came out for a few seconds. "Honey, these are very evil and nasty people. I have a plan that will get us away to safety. Are you sure that you are OK?"

"Yes. I am fine. They have not hurt me since that first phone call. They have me locked up in one cabin on this boat, but I am getting fed and….." The conversation abruptly ended as the line disconnected.

Chapter 21

Jeremy stared at the phone in his hand, unsure what his next move should be. He checked the chart to see if other boats appeared on the AIS chart plotter. AIS only identified boats within the line of sight and boats that turned on the transmitting function of AIS. He grabbed the binoculars and searched the horizon, but all he could see was the brilliant blue water. Not a single boat to be seen through the high-powered image-stabilizing binoculars.

Iona sailed for that mysterious heading in the ocean, about 75 miles from his current position. Jeremy was not sure what to expect when he got there. Checking the chart plotter again, he saw no other boats with AIS on the chart plotter within 20 miles. He turned on the radar. To his surprise, there appeared a target coming right for him. The radar measured the closest point of approach at 10 meters. This meant that the radar target was aimed right at him. The speed of the target at 40 knots suggested a powerful speedboat. The speedboat at 16 miles away closed the distance rapidly. It would be visible shortly and on him in less than half an hour. Jeremy needed to be ready. He put the remote starter in his life jacket pocket to be easily accessible. After all the planning, his confidence assured him he would control the outcome of this encounter.

He saw the speedboat now, bright red and traveling quickly towards him. Jeremy predicted the speedboat's arrival at the sailboat in less than 5 minutes. Jeremy checked to ensure that the Internet was working so that when he needed to use the remote BBQ starter, it would activate the explosion. Adrenaline pumped through his body, causing him to be totally alert and angry. He would need that anger directed at these assholes that had ruined his life and threatened Iona.

The speedboat pulled up beside *Iona.* He saw Iona, and she waved to him. Jeremy lowered the swim platform, and Iona hopped on board. They wrapped their arms around each other, and both cried. It started as a quiet sob, but then grew louder and louder as they squeezed each other tighter and tighter. "Everything will be fine now, Iona; we have each other, and I'm never letting go," said Jeremy between sobs.

The two sailors on board the red speed boat remained quiet as they watched the emotional reunion between Iona and Jeremy.

"Permission to come aboard." bellowed Julian.

Jeremy froze. Rick Mandel's words rang in his head. He called it correctly. Julian was behind everything. The surprise for Jeremy was that Julian was doing the dirty work rather than hiring thugs. When Jeremy didn't answer, Julian hopped on board.

"Thank you for bringing all this cargo to me," said Julian. "You almost scuttled the entire operation."

"Julian, you are an asshole," said Jeremy between clenched teeth. "Here's what is going to happen. I am going to launch the dinghy. Iona and I are going to head for the horizon. If you put up a fight, I will blow you and your cargo into dust."

Julian stared at Jeremy, took a step toward Iona, and reached out to grab her. Jeremy pulled out the remote BBQ starter with his thumb on the button. "Don't even think about it," said Jeremy. "I'm smart enough to know that once you have what you want, you will kill both of us. I will blow up all of us. Julian, I have nothing to lose. Iona, honey, can you lower the dinghy?"

Julian said. "I think not, Jeremy. I appreciate you letting me know about your plans to blow up my cargo, but I have deactivated your Starlink internet using a signal-jamming device. Your remote starter is useless."

Jeremy's face became red. He pressed the button and braced himself for the explosion. With a single movement, he picked up Iona to protect her from the impending explosion, and they both landed on the swim platform and covered their heads. In the millisecond before he thought of jumping into the water with Iona, he realized there would not be an explosion. It took a few more seconds of silence for everything to sink in. His plan failed. He was despondent.

"You two can get back up here now. I have very different

plans," said Julian. "The first task is to unload all this wonderful powder."

Iona and Jeremy re-entered the cockpit. Julian bound them together with zip-lock ties around their wrists and legs. Iona and Jeremy watched as Julian and another man unloaded the plastic bags full of cocaine onto their speedboat. It took about one hour. The quantity of bags astounded Jeremy, much more than he had imagined. Jeremy quickly calculated and estimated there must be approximately 1000 kilograms of cocaine. The value of this cargo challenged the normally fast-calculating arithmetic in his mind. He was certain that to keep the cocaine secret safe, Julian must ensure that Jeremy and Iona permanently became silenced.

Chapter 22

As the two men loaded the bags of cocaine from the front of the boat, Jeremy risked it was safe to talk with Iona without getting overheard. "Are you OK, honey?"

"Better now that I am with you," she said.

"I am getting the idea of what will happen to us," said Jeremy. "Julian will not allow us to go free on this boat. I don't think he has the guts to kill us with his bare hands. I met Rick Mandel before I left. He predicted Julian was behind all of this, and he was right. Rick says that Julian is a psychopath, highly intelligent, and addicted to cocaine. These three factors make him one of the most dangerous men he has ever met. I suspect he will throw us overboard. This is what modern-day pirates would do. People get lost at sea all the time with no obvious explanation."

"I came to the same conclusion," said Iona. "He has no empathy or sense of right or wrong. Throw in the cocaine factor, and he will do almost anything to preserve himself and his addiction."

"Tucked away in my inflatable life vest and yours, we have an AIS transmitter and an AIS receiver, which has a range of 4 miles." Said Jeremy. "Also tucked inside my inflatable life jacket is a small EPIRB. I got it a month ago."

"What's EPIRB," asked Iona.

"It's an Emergency Position Indicating Radio Beacon." Said Jeremy. "It transmits your position anywhere in the world as an emergency signal, but it takes 24 hours for the search and rescue team to get to you. I bought two of them. One for you, and one for me. I got them at the *safety at sea course* I did last month. Yours is at the captain's table. The closest country will contact Transport Canada as soon as it goes off. They will call the registered number to ensure it is not an accident. They will place this first call to your cell phone. Do you have your cell phone with you?"

"Ha ha, that is the first item they jettisoned." Said Iona.

Jeremy said. "They will direct the second phone call to my cellphone. If Julian answers it pretending he is me, what do you think he will say to them? Could you reach into my front right pocket and pull out my cell phone?"

Iona moved her two hands against the pocket so she could slide the cell phone up through the top opening. When a corner of the phone poked through, she could grab and remove it with her teeth. She transferred the phone to her bound hands. "What should I do with it now? Should I try making a call?"

Jeremy said. "Julian jammed the internet, so it won't work. Throw it as far away from the boat as you can."

Her two bound hands worked together as one. Iona lifted her hands above her head and launched the cell phone as far as possible. It landed on the swim platform and then bounced into the water. They both watched it sink on its way to the bottom of the ocean. The water was crystal clear, and they saw it descend slowly for the first ten feet, and then it disappeared.

Jeremy said. "You can retrieve your EBIRB from the captain's table. When two devices activate from the same vessel, it will be obvious to any search and rescue team that it was no accident."

They both thought about that for a minute. If Iona tried to pull a fast one, like saying that she had to go to the bathroom and grab it on the way, Julian and his helper would immediately be suspicious. Jeremy and Iona would have to wait for an opportunity before they could grab the 2nd EPIRB device. It was unlikely that Julian would know he had one buried in his inflatable life jacket, as it was a small new device that had not yet reached the mainstream market. The larger EPIRB version attached to boats in case of emergency had been on the market for years and was of proven value in saving lives. Thoughts of the EPIRB filled his mind when Julian appeared.

"I finished transferring the goods," said Julian. "I want you to understand that I respect you, Jeremy. I don't want you to take this personally, but I am a survivor. Nothing will stand in my way. You are a good person, Jeremy, but I also believe that you will stop at nothing to bring me down now that the truth about me is clear. I cannot let that happen. Unfortunately, Iona is involved, but it would be very detrimental if my story got out. I am about to disappear. No one is ever going to find me. One last thing. I need your EPIRB."

Jeremy's jaw dropped. His pulse quickened, and he stared at Julian silently. "I don't know what you're talking about," Jeremy said after a few seconds.

"Come on, Jeremy. First, there is no way you'd have a boat like this without having an EPIRB. Second, I know you are lying. You cannot lie successfully. I am an expert at reading people. There are certain physiological responses you cannot control. Like when I mentioned the EPIRB, your pupils dilated. Your eyes darted slightly to the left, and you hesitated before you answered with the lie. So, where is your EPIRB?"

Again defeated, Jeremy understood he was up against something he had never encountered before. Truly an evil force. A brief thought flashed across his mind. Maybe Julian thought he possessed only one EPIRB, and if Jeremy gave it to him, that would be the end of the discussion.

Jeremy sighed. "It's inside the captain's table."

Julian descended into the cabin, and opened the captain's table. He retrieved the yellow cylinder that housed the personal EPIRB meant for Iona. Julian placed it in his shirt pocket. "Huh," said Julian. "I thought it would be larger. Iona, where is your life jacket? I want you to put it on."

Julian cut her zip ties with the scissors he was carrying in his hands. He started with her ankles and cut the zip ties from her wrists. Iona descended the stairs into the main cabin. She removed the life jacket from the locker and put it on. Julian confused her. This was going against what she thought was about to happen. Maybe Julian was not a psychopath after all. Maybe they overreacted. Why would he ask for her to wear her life jacket if he planned on killing both of them?

Iona came up the stairs. The other man rested on a cushion in the cockpit by this time. Julian and the helper reached down as if to help Iona up the stairs and, in one smooth motion, threw her over the side of the boat. Iona screamed and landed with a splash. Her life jacket auto-inflated as she drifted away in the current, away from the boat.

Jeremy, at first, did not believe what happened. He struggled in his zip ties, but because they fixed the wrists and legs to the metal posts at the stern, he could not move. The ties cut into his wrists and ankles, but there was no pain, just blood as the ties dug into the tissue. "You sons of bitches!" Jeremy cried. "Go back and get her, you cowardly bastards," Jeremy yelled, every insult coming to his mind as he wriggled and fought with the zip ties. The two men simply stared at Jeremy wordlessly. After about five minutes, Jeremy stopped trying to move. His wrists and ankles were bleeding profusely. His voice, hoarse from yelling, caused the words to come out as whispers.

"Sorry, Jeremy, I did not mean it to be this way. I need this to look like the accidental sinking of your boat. When they find your body or what is left of them, the expectation from the coastguards would be that you were wearing your life jacket. All sailors wear life jackets while at sea these days, and I need this to look like an accident. You and Iona will probably survive for about 24 hours, and then you will succumb to dehydration or sharks. We will remove all the stopcocks from the boat so it will sink in 8000 meters of water, never to be seen again. If someone ever finds you, which is unlikely, all that will remain will be your life jacket. The coastguard will logically assume that the boat sank and not suspect this was deliberate." Julian pulled out a syringe and plunged it into Jeremy's neck. Jeremy looked at Julian incredulously as he tried to fight, sinking into a deep, black hole. Looking up at Julian, he saw no emotions on his face. There was no sadness. He saw no regret. A few seconds later, Jeremy passed out.

Chapter 23

Jeremy awoke surrounded by the ocean swells in a confused state. His life jacket was auto-inflated, which prevented him from drowning by keeping his head out of the water. The first thought that crossed his mind was that he would not survive over 24 hours. He slowly pieced together the events of the previous few hours. He thought about how he had failed Iona. His concern was not about his own life, only Iona's. During that trip on the sailboat from Toronto, he grew accustomed to the likelihood that his return to Toronto would never occur. He promised himself he would do anything possible to help Iona survive this. The EPIRB activated when the life vest inflated and flashed a red light. His AIS also flashed, but the signal would only travel along the line of sight, approximately 4 miles.

Jeremy fished in the pockets of the life jacket and pulled out his Garmin Inreach. He pressed the SOS button, hoping it could reach someone who could help him. He had little faith in this old technology, as the Garmin Inreach signal used satellites that were 30 years old. Inside the other pocket of a life jacket rested the AIS receiver. He turned it on. He looked for the AIS signal from *Iona*. Nothing appeared. He was getting bounced around in the ocean with the five-foot swells. When he reached the top of a swell, he looked across the horizon and saw nothing but more ocean swells. Jeremy glanced at the receiver and saw a signal. The icon on the receiver showed a man overboard, about 3 miles away, almost due east. Iona!

The sun was low on the horizon, setting in the west as Jeremy started swimming east. He estimated it could take him approximately three hours to get there, as swimming with the lifejacket blown up was difficult. Periodically, he rested and looked for the position of the AIS signal. He was getting closer. He kicked with his feet laying on his back. Swimming the backstroke with his arms forced his body to remain in that position. Darkness set in as the nighttime advanced. He used the stars to guide him, keeping him swimming in an easterly direction. He checked the AIS transponder and was now about 200 meters away from the signal. It took him a good deal of time to get this close. He called her name. When she didn't respond, he pulled out the whistle and blew loudly on the whistle. Tears started running down his face when he heard a whistle blowback in response. He blew his whistle again to let her know he was on his way, and within 10 minutes, he saw her floating between the waves.

They squeezed each other with such force they had difficulty breathing. They were both flowing with rivers of tears of happiness and joy. "I knew you would find me," said Iona through tears. "I didn't know why I knew this, but the belief was so strong, it has kept my spirits up, and here you are now."

"I switched on my EPIRB. With any luck, we will get rescued. We are about 200 miles offshore from one island in the Bahamas. My guess is that they won't start the search and rescue effort until the morning, so all we must do is stay alive until then," said Jeremy.

They held each other throughout the entire night. Jeremy remained awake the whole time, but Iona periodically slipped into a deep sleep. Jeremy cradled her head in his hands to cushion the effects of the waves. By morning, however, they were both fast asleep, floating in the water, but strapped together with their harnesses to avoid drifting apart. It was the whooping sound of the helicopter that woke up Jeremy. The helicopter hovered directly overhead. He lifted his hands and waved. He saw someone sitting in the helicopter's doorway. The swimmer-rescuer suddenly jumped into the water and swam over to them.

"Are you guys OK?" he asked.

Jeremy and Iona both nodded their heads. Everything happened quickly after that. They lowered a basket from the helicopter to the water, and the swimmer-rescuer put Iona into the basket. She was quickly pulled up into the helicopter. The helicopter lifted the swimmer-rescuer last after Jeremy was safely on board. The helicopter sped off towards the land.

After the one-hour flight, the helicopter landed in the field next to the small hospital in Georgetown, the Exumas. It was a small 10-12 bed hospital, the closest facility to the rescue site. The larger hospital in Nassau was 150 miles away, too far for the helicopter to refuel. Dr. Julie Rolle, the on-call physician for the day, examined Jeremy and Iona. She hooked them to an intravenous and placed them in hospital beds. They were both dehydrated and exhausted. She gave them sedatives, and they fell into a deep sleep for 12 hours. When Jeremy woke up, he found himself handcuffed to the bed.

Chapter 24

Iona was sitting in an interrogation room in the police station in Georgetown, the Exumas. The officers had interrogated her for the last six hours. Jeremy, now handcuffed to the bed, remained hooked up to the intravenous in the hospital. The police officers did not believe her story. It did not take them long to call the police in Toronto to find out that Jeremy skipped bail following charges of murder. The bail conditions prohibited him from leaving the country.

"There is something else," said Officer Samuels as he spoke with Iona. "There's a warrant out for Jeremy's arrest for assault and battery of Reverend Rowen, who I believe you both know. The reverend, brutally beaten in his church, alleges Jeremy did this. The extradition agreement facilitates criminal transfers to Canada. I consulted our legal team, and the Royal Bahamas Police Force plans to pursue this option." It was obvious to Iona that they had no intention of going after Julian Yacoby based on a baffling story from a criminal and his wayward wife.

Iona walked down the street after they released her from the police station. She tried to focus on the next steps. Exhaustion prevented her from thinking clearly. She walked into the Peace and Plenty Hotel. She booked a room there for the night. The first phone call she made was to Michael, Jeremy's criminal lawyer. She spoke with him on the phone for the next hour. He listened without saying a word.

"I'm coming down on the next flight to Georgetown. Make sure that he says nothing to the police," said Michael.

Michael met Iona the following afternoon in the hotel's lobby. He spent the morning discussing with the police and their lawyers. "I've heard a lot of crazy stories in my time. I have never heard a story quite like yours and Jeremy's. You are right. They do not believe you. We have *Iona's* AIS tracking, so we confirm Jeremy sailed where he said. We also tracked his cell phone's GPS and lost that signal around when you threw it in the water. The Ontario Provincial Police and their counsel informed me they lost *Iona's* signal about 10 miles from where the helicopter saved you. They suspected the boat sank in 8000 meters of water. This all fits in with your story."

Iona said, "They are planning on transferring Jeremy to His Majesty's Prison Fox Hill in Nassau as soon as the doctors give him medical clearance. I worry that with Julian's reach, Jeremy's life would be in danger in that prison. There are all kinds of drug dealers there who would do anything to get some of Julian's 100% cocaine. He is a lot safer in the hospital."

Michael said, "You must understand my position. I am an officer of the court, and I cannot encourage you or even suggest that you do anything illegal. However, I think you are right. Within a few days of prison, they would likely knife Jeremy. The Bahamas tries its best, but there still is a lot of corruption here. They can buy off prison guards, and some officials accept bribes. I had some past dealings with this country, and I know this for a fact."

"What am I going to do?" asked Iona.

"My advice would be to meet with the doctor. Try to delay the transfer as long as possible. I would also recommend hiring a bodyguard while in the hospital. He will need some protection," said Michael. "I'm going to fly back to Toronto and see what I can dig up about Reverend Rowen. I am certain that he is part of this. I'm not sure there's much more I can do here. I don't have any legal rights in the Bahamas, but I wanted to meet with you so that you understand where I am coming from."

Iona was despondent. She hoped that Michael would have the solutions to all these legal issues and that Iona and Jeremy would fly back to Toronto on the next flight. It was going to be a lot more complicated than that. She returned to the hospital to speak with the doctor and Jeremy to discuss her meeting with Michael. Iona ran into Dr. Julie Rolle, the doctor assigned to look after them when they first arrived at the medical facility. Julie exited the small examining room. "Iona, I need to speak with you. Someone tried to kill Jeremy."

Iona bolted into Jeremy's hospital room just around the corner. Jeremy's door hung on one hinge and was askew. The room was empty. The ruffled, unmade bed suggested a recent skirmish. There was blood everywhere on the floor. The empty handcuffs on the bedpost dangled. Jeremy was gone.

"Oh my God!" cried Iona. "Where have they taken him, Dr. Rolle?"

"He's OK. He's safe," said Dr. Rolle. "Come and sit down in my office. I'll fill you in on what happened. Please call me Julie."

Iona cried. This had been too much all at once. Now someone tried to kill Jeremy. When was this nightmare going to end? She hugged Dr. Rolle, who whispered. "He is safe." Iona couldn't stop crying and stained Julie's purple scrub suit.

"Julie," said Iona, as she gained control of her emotions. "Please, tell me what happened."

"A man I have never seen before came into his room as I talked to Jeremy an hour ago. He was a skinny white man. Blue tattoos covered his arms like the kind they do in prison. He told me to leave and that he had business to discuss with Jeremy. I said I wouldn't leave, and he picked me up and shoved me through the door. That is how it broke. Fortunately, my brother Brian, a general surgeon, just finished an operation. He was on his way to the cafeteria. As soon as he noticed the trouble, he rushed into Jeremy's room. He tackled the man who had a knife. Jeremy kicked the tattooed man in the face. I think his nose got broken because there was blood everywhere. The knife flew across the room, and the tattooed man took off."

"Where is Jeremy now?" asked Iona.

"I don't know," said Julie. "But Brian did his fellowship training in Toronto. He heard about Jeremy's exceptional laparoscopic surgery skills from other doctors. Brian talked to him at a meeting. He suspected Jeremy wouldn't remember. My brother is certain that Jeremy would never do what they accused him of. Did you know Jeremy's arrest for murder was international news?

"We have been in the Bahamas all our lives. Brian and I went to medical school in New York City with the agreement that we would return to work in the Bahamas for at least 5 years. The government funded the training. Brian did most of his surgical training in New York City and one year in Toronto. I did family medicine training. We have no intention of leaving the Bahamas, but we often offer outreach medicine in remote areas. Understanding all the islands, my brother and I will conceal Jeremy somewhere where no one will locate him. Of that, I am certain. Let me call him on the satellite phone. Brian encrypted it and made the phone secure."

Julie called the number. After a brief conversation, she

passed the phone to Iona.

"Jeremy!" Iona said.

"Iona," said Jeremy. "That was a close one! It was only because of the fast thinking of Julie and Brian that I could escape. They are telling me we cannot trust the police. There are still a lot of drugs and trafficking in the Bahamas. Many of the police officers are getting kickbacks."

"What are we going to do now?" asked Iona.

"Iona, you must leave the Bahamas as quickly as possible. It's too dangerous to stay. Fly to Nassau and go to the Canadian embassy to get a new passport, then fly home. I think you can do more at home to help than staying here. Brian says that you can contact me on this phone. It is untraceable. We'll talk every day. I love you."

"I love you too. We'll get through this, I am certain. We'll talk soon." Iona hung up the phone.

After the phone call, Julie went online to look for flights to Nassau for Iona. "There's a flight to Nassau on Maker's airline in 60 minutes. Let's get you on it!" said Julie. "We'll pay for it when we get to the airport. I'll drive!"

Chapter 25

It was 1992, and Brian and Julie Rolle were 12 and 10 years old. They looked after themselves. They played in the jungle near the mangrove river. Brian pretended to be a hunter with his bow and arrow. The only problem was that the arrow tip had one of those suction cup ends for kids, so they would not hurt themselves while they played. Julie crawled across the mangroves to get the birds to fly, and then Brian, the hunter, pulled back the sting on his bow and pretended to shoot them as they flew by. He didn't want to use his arrows because they would be difficult to find in the jungle. He was not a very good shot, anyway.

"Get away from me, you pervert!" Julie screamed. Brian could see her through the mangroves and hopped onto a mangrove tree branch for a better view. A man, one of his father's friends, taunted Julie. They were on a patch of solid ground amongst the water and mangrove roots.

"You are growing up to be quite the cutie," the man said. "You are just at the age when you should learn how to please a man like me. I'm doing you a favor." He was holding her arm and gently stroking her black, curly hair. Julie was precocious, with small breasts developing on her chest. Her mother had explained the monthly cycle, which would likely begin shortly. The man stopped stroking her hair and started unbuckling his belt.

Brian saw all this from the mangrove tree branch and silently sat directly above them. He pulled out his arrow and loaded it onto the bow. He pulled back the bowstring and fired the arrow. The suction cup hit the man with such force it caused the arrow to stick to the man's forehead. He cried out a startled scream and let go of Julie. Julie hopped up on the mangrove roots and raced towards the river, heading for their kayak. Brian fired two arrows at the man. One missed, but the next hit him on the side of the neck. Brian heard him howling as he jumped off the tree and headed for the kayak. Julie was already there with the paddles. Brian hopped on the back seat as they paddled back to the Eco Lodge as quickly as possible.

Brian and Julie realized they had to look out for one another. Their mother disliked visiting the Eco Lodge. Their father would bring them, and he told them it would be good for them to spend time with nature. It was the only time they would spend with their father, who was always away on "business". Even these times were too much to spend with the man they both despised. He told them they were stupid and did not understand the ways of the world. If Julie and Brian got too close to him, they feared he would direct his anger toward them and beat them. Their father accused them of always getting in the way, and he would yell at them for the most trivial reasons. He spent most of the days in the eco-friendly resort meeting with his business partners and spent as little time as possible with them. This was satisfactory for Brian and Julie because there were many interesting things to do at the Eco Lodge.

The Eco Lodge was a stunning hotel constructed on the side of the rock. There were multiple waterfalls and water slides they explored. The water funneled into a large natural spring swimming pool, which was cool in the hot Dominican Republic sun. Often, they would hike up the mountain with their inner tubes and float down the stream. At some point, they would come across a small waterfall, fly, be catapulted by the force of the water, and land in the quiet pond at the bottom. Usually, they fell off the inner tubes when they landed. They would then climb back on their inner tubes as they continued their adventure downstream to the Eco Lodge.

The deserted Eco Lodge mysteriously had no guests. Approximately 20 hotel employees occupied the hotel and several of their father's business associates. The hotel was always empty. One day, looking for something to do, they counted all the hotel rooms. There were over 100 rooms. As far as they could tell, no one had ever stayed in the hotel rooms. There were at least 3 bars that were well stocked with bottles of alcohol, but they had seen no one sitting on the bar stools. The restaurant where they ate was usually empty except for the two of them. The kitchen staff was very nice. They would bring them whatever they wanted. The staff spoke Spanish, and they both rapidly learned the language.

Brian and Julie had been visiting here for many years. They

sometimes spent up to two months exploring the secret places. They took a speedboat for the 30-minute ride across the Bay of Samana in the Dominican Republic to get to the Eco Lodge. Then they hopped in an inflatable dinghy up the mangrove-lined river for 2 miles to a small dock. Arriving by horseback, they followed a narrow path to the Eco Lodge. The builders constructed the hotel on the side of the granite mountain and used stone to build the rooms. It blended into the jungle and mountain, so seeing the Eco Lodge from the Bay of Samana was difficult.

5 years later, after their father died, Brian and Julie discovered the true purpose of Eco Lodge. Their father's accountant sat in their living room in their expansive house in February Point near Georgetown, the Bahamas.

"Your father's finances were complicated," said Gavi Murdoch. Your father was involved in drug trafficking, particularly cocaine, from Colombia to the US.

Bryan said. "Julie and I suspected as much. We were not close to our father; we hated him. As we grew older, we did not hide this from him. We have absolutely no interest in his business or money. Our plan is to sell this beautiful house to finance our education. We will both become doctors and do some good to rectify some of the harm he has done."

Gavi sighed. "Since his death, bilateral agreements have

frozen many of his assets between the Bahamian government and the United States. The Drug Enforcement Agency has been tracking him for years. Your father moved his operation to Haiti and the Dominican Republic after the drug trafficking crackdowns in the Bahamas. This house is in your mother's name, so you might be OK, but you must be careful. My advice would be to hang on to the house. The government would ask fewer questions. You would not want this house to be seized as well.

"I wanted to discuss the Eco Lodge in the Dominican Republic with you. They financed this lodge solely to produce income, so it would appear to be from a legitimate source. We have never seen such a complex financing arrangement. To simplify, there is a pool of money, perhaps close to $500 million, in a bank account in Panama. They set it up so that no one could access that bank account. No one can trace this account back to your father or you. We have set up a series of complex Visa card transactions so that a group of fake tourists comes every year for two weeks. 1800 fake Visa card accounts draw $7000 for their 2 weeks stay. This allows $12,600,000 to come to the Eco Lodge to finance the hotel, pay the staff, and do the maintenance. Here's the thing, no one has ever come to the hotel as a guest."

Brian raised his eyebrows. "Why not just sell the lodge or tell the DEA that this is the asset of my father?"

"There is no way to link your father with this hotel. They set it up to run like this forever," said Gavi. "You and Julie have always been the legitimate owners of this hotel. I suspect that's why your father kept bringing you along when he was doing business there. It is yours to do whatever you wish with it.

"My advice is to keep the operation going as they have set it up so it would be very hard, if not impossible, to dismantle."

After the accountant left, Julie and Brian had time to discuss what they had learned. At just 17 and 15 years old, they had matured beyond their years because of the necessity of survival. The realization that their father was a bad person made them shed no tears when they learned of his death. They were neither sad nor aggrieved. They talked about their lack of feelings for their father often. His uncaring attitude towards their mother caused her to leave a few years ago. Since then, they have been taking care of themselves.

Brian and Julie grew to be quite fond of the staff at the Eco Lodge. It was as if they adopted them as their children and welcomed them as family. This was the main reason they enjoyed going there for all those years. The staff would care for them for at least 2 months a year. They would feed them, talk with them, and genuinely care about them. They brought them to their homes. Brian and Julie became friends with their children, parents, and grandparents. The staff greeted them with love and affection when they visited their homes. It was as though the staff knew their father deprived Julie and Brian of love because of his uncaring attitude, and they were trying to make it up to them.

"It sounds like the Eco Lodge will continue to be our happy and secret place forever," said Julie with a smile.

Chapter 26

Jeremy woke up in the presidential suite at the Eco Lodge. It had taken about 20 hours by boat to get there from Georgetown after narrowing evading death from the tattooed assassin. He arrived in the middle of the night after a transfer to a smaller speedboat to get across the 15-mile bay. An all-terrain vehicle transported him to the Eco Lodge after navigating a mangrove-lined river in the dark. Brian had convinced him it was the safest place to hide. The Eco Lodge was in the jungle of the Dominican Republic, and few, except those that worked there, knew the Eco Lodge existed. Brian and Julie had known and trusted these people for over 30 years. The staff was loyal. Nobody would ever find Jeremy.

The grounds and the hotel were beautiful and immaculately groomed. They trimmed the grass and planted beautiful flowers in the garden. The presidential suite was a large room with a king-size bed. There was an enormous bathroom the size of his old apartment when he was in medical school. Someone brought fresh fruit on a platter and a thermos full of fresh coffee. He took this outside and sat at a small table on the balcony. From here, he saw across the Bay of Samana. It astounded him that nobody was aware that this place existed. It was, without a doubt, the nicest hotel he had ever visited.

Jeremy turned on the satellite phone Brian had given him and called. "Hello Michael, this is Jeremy. I'm calling from an untraceable satellite phone. I just wanted to let you know I am safe."

Initially, there was silence at the other end of the line. "Jeremy," said Michael, "I was worried sick. Iona told me about the difficulty you encountered in the medical facility. Iona is coming back from Nassau tonight. I'll pick her up at the airport. There's going to be a heap of press. You are creating quite a stir in the international news. Where are you?"

Jeremy said, "I'm not entirely sure, and perhaps it's best that you do not know either. The physicians from the clinic helped me escape, and I will remain in hiding until I decide my next move."

Michael said, "Jeremy, it's impossible to stay hidden in this digital world. Your picture is all over the Internet. I'd like to get you to safety."

Jeremy said, "Julian planned to stay hidden. I'm not sure how he planned on doing that, but he sees me as a threat to his plans. The only way I will remain safe is to get to Julian and disrupt his plans permanently. Besides, there is no way that they will treat me fairly in the legal system in Canada because it is true, I assaulted the reverend and his co-worker. From my perspective, the attack was justified, as they were the ones that detained me. I suspect I would be dead now if I had not escaped.

The other legal concern for me is that there is no proof that the drug production facility beneath the church existed. The only truths are the injuries that I inflicted on those two criminals. My best hope is for you and Iona to discredit the reverend. My guess is that he's addicted to cocaine and fentanyl. Now that the drug production facility has shut down, he will, at some point, run out of supply. The biggest lever we have on him will be his addiction and craving."

Michael said, "I've got our private investigator tailing him, so we will see where that leads. Let's talk in a few days."

Chapter 27

John Papadopoulos drank rum at his usual table in the Antigua Yacht Club in Falmouth Harbour. He sat with Julian. "Your new name is Andy Smith," John said. "Here is your package of documents. These include birth certificates, visa cards, American Express, banking information, Bahama passport and more. Do a Google search of Andy Smith, and you'll get hundreds of hits. Your identity just blends in with at least 30 of them. There is no way anyone can trace your name back to your former life."

"And all of this cost $10 million?" asked Julian. "How do I know that my secret is safe with you?"

"Identity theft is common practice these days. Identity theft that is untraceable costs a lot of money. The rest of the money was used to smooth the transaction for that private island in the Bahamas. It used to be owned by an infamous Bahamian drug dealer, so we took careful precautions to cover our tracks. I paid off some government officials so they would not ask too many questions. We bought the bankrupt Crystal Cruises Line using one of your numbered Panamanian companies for pennies on the dollar. The island now belongs to Crystal Cruises Line. The construction of your villa will cost another $10 million. You will need 24/7 guards for about $1,000,000 per year. No one is going to find you, thanks to me."

"What if someone recognizes my face?" asks Julian. "Don't I need plastic surgery or something?"

"The best way to change your appearance is to grow a beard and shave your head. It is highly unlikely that anyone will recognize you after a few years. Look at me," John said. "I've been hiding for over 10 years, and no one has recognized me. I live in public a lot more than you are planning. Once you're in a new place, someone will not recognize you partly because your new life is completely out of context with what anyone is expecting.

"It turns out that you are much more likely to be recognized by the way you walk, or perhaps the way your eyebrows raise before you answer a question, for example. Often it is the slight mannerism that gives away identity. They are easy to change once you realize your unique mannerisms."

John added. "Part of that fee goes to Melody. Speaking of the angels in heaven, there she is."

Melody was a gorgeous woman. She waved to them as she made her way towards their table. She wore brown khaki shorts that led down to her tanned, athletic legs. The tight-fitting shorts outlined fulsome hips. She had the lithe figure of a runner. Every man in the bar turned for a quick glance as she wore a white button-down collared T-shirt that showed just enough cleavage. Embroidered on her right breast was 'Melody' and on her left breast, 'A King's

Ransom'. At about 5'9", she was tall. She tied her brown hair into a ponytail at the back. She gracefully glided over to Julian and John.

"Andy, I'd like you to meet your mannerism coach." Said John. "Let's go to the boat for your first lesson."

Julian lay on his back. Beside him, Melody slept. She breathed softly, deep in her dreams. He had to admit that was probably the best sex ever. After leaving the Antigua Yacht Club, John brought them to his mega yacht. "You will stay here for a week while Melody turns you into a new man," John explained.

Melody said that the first lesson in mannerisms involved pleasing a woman. She corrected a few clumsy moves that Julian claimed he had perfected after years of practice in the bedroom. She said, "You must make a woman feel like she is the most important thing in your life. You must go slowly. It is OK to ask the woman what she wants you to do."

Julian followed her instructions with what she wanted, resulting in mind-blowing sex. Sure, the cocaine beforehand helped them achieve ecstasy levels that he never knew were possible, but she brought him places out of this world. He lay there covered in a thin layer of sweat, thinking he could enjoy this newfound freedom. This was certainly better than slogging it out as an orthopedic surgeon, embedding new hips and knees into unappreciative geriatric patients.

The week went by quickly. Melody gave him instructions on how to walk differently. She pointed out certain intonations he would make when he talked and how he could easily change those. She showed him how his hand motions usually revealed what he was thinking and how to move his hands differently when speaking. To grow a beard and shave his head, she assured him, would be enough. These things would change his appearance, along with the changes in his mannerisms, so no one would recognize him. Best of all, she revealed the secrets to having the best sex. Julian awoke on the day the week finished, and she had left. There was an imprint in the bed where she had slept, but she was not there. The mannerism lessons were over.

Chapter 28

Jack sat in his car, watching Reverend Rowen through his window in the sitting room. It was a cloudy but warm evening. Jack Mulligan was the private investigator Michael hired to discover what was happening with the reverend. Michael asked him to photograph the reverend and report any information that would implicate him. So far, things have been boring. They released the reverend from the hospital about two weeks ago. He required a splenectomy for a ruptured spleen from the brutal attack that the reverend alleged was the work of Jeremy. They administered treatment to him for a mild concussion. Jack took pictures from his car using the telescopic lens. Through the telescopic lens, he saw a clear view of the sitting room through the window. The reverend and his wife sat in the sitting room, reading. He captured images of that. The wife got up, kissed the reverend on the top of his head, and then headed up the stairs, presumably to bed.

After a few minutes, the reverend got up and pushed a painting aside. Behind the painting exposed a safe. Jack snapped a photo of that. He took a series of pictures a millisecond apart so that the combination to the safe appeared sequentially. The reverend looked left, then right, to ensure no one lurked around. Assured of privacy, he then opened the safe. It was dark in the safe, but through the telescopic lens, there appeared to be several plastic bags that were full of white powder. The reverend took a small stash in a small bag and closed the safe. Jack took many pictures of this.

The reverend then sat out on his porch, attempting to hide behind the trellis so no one passing by could see him. He looked up and down the street and saw there was no one. Using the telescopic lens, the angle of view allowed Jack to observe the reverend place a line of cocaine on the armrest of the Muskoka chair. With a small straw, he removed from his top right shirt pocket, he inhaled the line into his left nostril. Jack captured all of this with his camera. After a few minutes elapsed, the reverend stood up and returned to the house. Jack saw him locking the door and headed up the stairs, presumably to join his wife in bed.

Jack could not believe his luck. After all his years of sleuthing, he had captured nothing so clearly damaging. Who would have thought that an upstanding reverend would be a cocaine user? He loaded the images into a zip file and e-mailed them to Michael. He then called Michael. "You won't believe what I just caught on camera," Jack said. "Open up the files that I just sent you."

While Michael opened the file on his smartphone, he told Jack, "You must keep this completely confidential. Jeremy's life is in danger, and no one can ever know I sent you to spy on the reverend.

"Holy shit!" cried Michael. "These photos are incredibly

damaging. If these ever get out, I see an invasion of privacy lawsuit. This is not something that an officer of the court can legally be part of. Let me think about what to do with these. Whatever else, do not tell anyone about this. Can you destroy the photos from your camera to prevent them from being subpoenaed later?"

"No worries, boss. With a button click, those pictures never happened from this camera," said Jack.

Iona was looking through the pictures that Michael had sent her. Michael explained it was important that no one ever traced the pictures back to him. She was to delete the e-mail and the contents immediately after downloading the pictures. She must tell no one that it came from him. Although Michael had no suggestions for proceeding, Iona had an idea. She learned a fair amount about drug addiction from her psychotherapy practice. Foremost for an addict is to get the drug. For some addicts, it meant stealing; for others, it involved lying; for others, cheating; and for the reverend, she was going to get him to tell the truth to exonerate Jeremy.

Chapter 29

Julie and Brian Rolle were scouring the Internet, looking for clues about where Julian could hide. There were over 700 islands, and he could be on any of them if he was in the Bahamas. Brian suspected Julian was in the Bahamas because of the vicinity to where Julian had taken off the cocaine from Jeremy's boat. If that logic was correct, it was possibly an island in the Exumas. There were 15 islands sold in the last five years. Incredulously, the most recent sale was to a cruise company. Their father had used this island as a drug warehousing facility 25 years earlier. It was seized by the DEA and handed back to the Bahamian government. They sold the island to a private investor after dismantling the warehousing structures.

The private investor had put it up for sale five years ago, and Crystal Cruises Lines had bought the island a few months ago. They advertised the island as having deep water access, which is why it might be attractive for a cruise company. However, Brian was familiar with the island and knew that the deepest waters were 12 feet at low tide. The closest any cruise ship would ever get to this island would be about 20 miles away, requiring at least 30 feet of depth without running aground. This made it impractical for a cruise ship to stop there to transfer guests for an afternoon of barbeque and drinking.

Julie asked. "Wouldn't it be ironic if someone converted our father's island back to a drug facility?"

"I agree it looks suspicious, doesn't it? Why would any legitimate cruise company buy an island to which they had no access? Look at this," said Brian, pointing to the internet page on the computer. "Crystal Cruises Lines went bankrupt in 2022. An investor bought the company a few months ago."

Early the next day, Hector, their pilot, flew Julie and Brian over the Exumas. He took Julie and Brian up in his well-maintained single-engine Piper Cherokee, over 40 years old. They used this plane whenever they flew out to the islands to give medical care for their medical outreach program. This time, however, they were going on a reconnaissance mission to look at the island. The island of interest was Leaf Cay, a 15-acre island with three white sandy beaches. It was two miles east of Staniel Cay, a popular island for sailors to visit. Leaf Cay was 75 miles southeast of Nassau and 48 miles from Georgetown. There was a helipad. Underwater cables from Staniel Cay connected the island to the main power grid of the Bahamas Electric Company.

There was a red powerboat tied up at the dock. There were a few buildings on the property. They saw nobody walking around, but they might have missed them as they flew high above the island.

Hector suggested, "Why don't we land at Staniel Cay airport

and then rent a powerboat and have a closer look at the island?"

"Great idea," said both Brian and Julie in unison. They laughed at their concurring comment.

It took about 5 minutes to get from Staniel Cay to Leaf Cay by the Boston Whaler trawler they rented for 3 hours. They first circumnavigated the island before coming to the dock. They had not yet spotted anyone on the island. The red speedboat remained tied to the dock, showing there would be someone nearby. They tied their Boston whaler to the dock. The dock was about 100 feet long. A large black man who wore camouflage, heavy army boots and a helmet marched quickly down towards them. He was carrying a rifle.

"Hold it right there!" He shouted. "This is private property, and you are trespassing. Get back on your trawler and leave."

Brian, Julie, and Hector stopped in their tracks. "We thought this island was for sale," lied Brian. "We were checking out the 3 beaches because we have someone who may be interested in purchasing it."

"I have news for you," shouted the man with the gun. "This island sold months ago, and the new owner does not want anyone to be here, so leave."

They hopped on their Boston Whaler and headed back to Staniel Cay. As they flew back to Georgetown, Brian said, "The only reason for armed guards is if you have a reason to hide something."

Julie said, "That's got to be the place, Brian. We know all the islands around here, and that was one of the strangest encounters we've ever seen. Whenever we visited any other island, they always greeted us like old friends, even when they didn't want us. I've seen nothing like this before. Nobody else has armed guards. Remember when we landed on Half Moon Cay, owned by the Carnival Cruise Company? They asked us to leave, but they were nice about it. They even asked if we were thirsty and offered bottled water to take with us."

Julian, aka Andy Smith, watched as the Cherokee Piper flew overhead. It seemed to do a semicircle around the island as if looking for something. He would have to be extra vigilant, at least at the beginning of this new life. Julian thought it might be possible that the story about looking to purchase the island for a client could be true. But a simple Google search of Leaf Cay would have revealed that Crystal Cruises line bought the island two months ago. No real estate agent he had ever dealt with would have made a mistake like that. In the meantime, he would double the guards and expedite the construction of his new villa. He put too much effort into this plan for it to be derailed. The thought of Jeremy came to his mind. That lucky cat literally had nine lives. The next time he ran into him, and he was certain he would, Julian would ensure he used up all his life.

Chapter 30

Iona took the direct approach with the reverend. He agreed to meet her in the church office. She told the reverend that she felt awful about how Jeremy had treated him. Iona also explained that she didn't understand why Jeremy had been acting so strange over the past few months and hoped to seek his advice. She quietly waited for him outside his rectory office in a small waiting room, flipping through gardening magazines.

"Iona," said the reverend as he approached her, "I am so sorry that I am late. Since getting out of the hospital, everything has taken just a little longer. Let's go into my office."

After sitting on the opposite side of the desk from the reverend, Iona began to cry. To make her anguish look authentic, she practiced in front of a mirror. Iona's sobs intensified, causing the reverend to leave his desk and embrace her. She rested her head against his shoulders. She only stopped after a few minutes and after many kind words of consolation. "There, there Iona. No need to cry. Everything will be alright. Don't worry."

When Iona was in medical school, she decided she wanted to practice psychotherapy and improve the mental health of at-risk patients. This was a needed service. Only a few therapists had the training to talk with patients and listen to all their problems. She did not hesitate when presented with the chance to do a master's thesis, adding two more years to her medical school journey. The premise of her thesis was *"How subtle seduction techniques used by women affect the mental health of men."* This involved a lot of interviews with men and women, but she also tested some principles herself.

Every Saturday night, she visited different singles bars and clubs around the city for six months. Her goal would be to use subtle seduction techniques to see how they affected a 'target'. As things intensified, she continued to escalate the sexual tension, amplifying these techniques. Just as the target became confident that he was in for a night of great sex and got ready to take her back to his place, she slipped away. She then waited by her phone for the inevitable phone call. The target might call within a few minutes; sometimes, the next morning; other times, a week later, but invariably, they all called.

When they called, the targets' reactions fell into three major categories. Those who blamed themselves for putting her off and scaring her away, those who were legitimately confused and didn't understand why she left, and those who were angry wanted to let her know how they felt. Iona had measured responses depending on the reaction. Ultimately, she reigned in their emotions and gained back their confidence. After some prompting, they let her learn what seduction techniques worked well and what didn't. She took careful notes of these conversations and used them for her research.

She determined that seduction was all about maintaining mystery. By using words carefully, she applied intonation with hesitation at the most effective moments. She talked to the target like he was the most interesting and handsome man on the face of the planet. To enhance her skills, she practiced using powerful tools like eye-locking, playing with her hair, and touching her lips with her fingers. She learned exactly when to touch his arm and let the touch linger for a fraction too long. Just as things got very intense, she would leave; but not before she made sure he had her phone number in his cell phone.

Since meeting Jeremy 25 years ago, she worried she was out of practice but was confident that the male species had evolved little since she published her thesis. Experience played in her favor because she treated many male and female patients who fell prey to these seduction techniques. Many of these patients needed therapy for anxiety and anger management.

Iona let go of the reverend after squeezing him against herself for perhaps too long. She kept her eyes glued to his, maintaining the stare while she wiped off an imaginary speck of dust from the right side of his face. She traced her finger along his arm. "So muscular," she whispered. "And to think that you suffered so much because of Jeremy. I intend to make this up to you, reverend. Let me make you dinner so we can talk more privately."

The reverend became speechless for a moment. He hadn't felt like this for many years. Previously, when he served as a younger reverend, he had a few affairs with young women who sought his help. On those few occasions when the young women poured out their problems to him, the sessions ended with him sleeping with them. Later, he began understanding the imbalance of power between a reverend and a young woman with problems. He then took precautions to avoid getting into this situation. Iona was different. She was a mature and beautiful woman and needed his help. The reverend told himself that he was up for the task.

The reverend took a moment to organize his ideas. "Why don't you come over to my house tonight," he said. "My wife has gone to Orangeville to visit her sister for several days, so we will have plenty of privacy to talk about things."

"Perfect," said Iona. "I'll make Chateau Briand, baked potatoes, a nice assortment of vegetables and Bearnaise sauce. See you at 7." She kissed him lightly on the cheek but held it there a bit too long. Looking into his eyes, she recognized the enraptured gaze she had seen with the targets years before. She smiled as she walked away. She had not lost her magic seductive powers.

"Michael, I need some advice," Iona said as she conversed with him on the phone. I have a general plan, but I think I require some advice on how to finesse this. My plan is simple. I will remove the cocaine from his safe. I will keep it hidden from him. His craving for the drug will be so intense that he will do whatever it takes, including informing us of the truth.

"I don't know about this, Iona. This sounds risky. I'll send our private investigator to take pictures. If we have at least your consent, I don't believe there will be any privacy concerns should we need to use the photos in a courtroom setting. I'll come along as well in case things go south," said Michael.

Iona and the reverend sat at the dining room table at the farthest end of the living room. The preparation for dinner had gone perfectly. She cooked the Chateau Briand roast with just enough pink, better than any fancy restaurant. They finished their first bottle of wine. The reverend had been pouring wine into Iona's wineglass, but she was pouring it down the sink when he was not watching as she prepared dinner. She parked her car down the street about a block away, as no parking spots were closer.

She said to the reverend, "Would you mind getting another bottle of wine from my car? It's parked down the street. While you do that, I'll clear these dishes and get dessert ready with coffee."

He gave her one of those 'I would do anything for you' looks that she was familiar with, and she silently shuddered. Maybe she had overdone it with the seduction techniques, and she thought to herself as he left the house to get the wine. She slipped into the living room. Pushing the picture aside, she dialed the combination she had memorized from the photos the private investigator had given her. Upon opening the safe, she identified three one-kilogram bags of cocaine/remifentanil mix. She removed the drugs and placed them in the large purse for this purpose. After closing the safe, she put the picture back in place. She then did what she had always done after a successful mission. She got ready to leave. As she opened the front door, she saw the reverend coming up the sidewalk. There was no way she could leave without being seen.

"You look like you're getting ready to leave, darling," said the reverend as he entered the house. The reverend looked different. His eyes were bloodshot, and his pupils dilated. The reverend was darting his eyes around the room. His agitation caused his legs to move up and down as a nervous tic. It was obvious to Iona that he had likely done a line of cocaine/remifentanil while on his way to get the wine.

"Yes, reverend. It's been lovely, but I must go," said Iona.

"I know that you have the hots for me. I can tell. I wasn't born yesterday." He reached over to grab her arm, and she twisted away.

"You old fool, keep your disgusting hands off of me," shouted Iona.

He grabbed her by the hair and hit her across her face. Iona fell to the floor. Iona moaned softly in pain. Her nose was bleeding. "There is no way I'm going to let you out of here without me giving you what you came for," whispered the reverend into her ear. "This is going to be the best day of your life." He started unbuckling his pants.

Iona rolled over on her back and seductively spread her legs. The reverend leaned over to take advantage of her change in attitude. She lifted her foot and kicked him in the crotch with such a violent force that it lifted him off the ground. Howling in pain beside Iona, he came crashing down to the floor. He rolled around the floor uncontrollably, stopping only to vomit forcibly, causing the vomitus to fly across the room to land on the adjacent wall. He screamed relentlessly.

Iona was unsteady on her feet as she went to the front door to escape. When she opened the door, two police officers ran up the walkway towards the house with their guns drawn. Three police cruisers lined the street with their blue lights flashing. Michael, right behind them, ran as fast as possible. She collapsed in his arms the moment that he reached her.

Chapter 31

Iona sat on the emergency room gurney, drinking orange juice. The ER doctor told her that the X-rays showed no damage or broken bones in her nose. The doctor found that she had minor contusions on her cheek where the reverend had hit her. Michael had not left her side after driving her to the hospital.

"We got everything on video," said Michael. "The police are charging him with sexual assault."

"The reverend will not survive 24 hours without his cocaine/remifentanil potion," said Iona. "I have seen it before in some of my patients. Their cravings will be intense for a cocaine hit. The narcotic withdrawal will cause him terrible abdominal pain, tachycardia, and cardiac arrhythmias. Sometimes the withdrawal symptoms are severe, which can cause death from cardiorespiratory collapse."

"We already reached out to Dr. Rick Mandel, whom you know well. He is on his way to the prison to meet with the reverend. As you know, he is an addiction specialist. An hour ago, he said the reverend has to continue with the cocaine/remifentanil while dealing with legal matters. It turns out that about 80% of inmates in prison have substance abuse or addiction. Illegal drug use in the prisons caused a huge spike in deaths, so the government allows inmates to continue drug use, but only under medical supervision.

"The best part is that the reverend came clean with his involvement in the entire drug production facility below his church. He confessed to planting the 30 doses of remifentanil in Jeremy's parked car one night when it was in the driveway. He hid the drugs in the bumper. The police did not release that information to anyone, so they are confident that he is telling them the truth."

"Does that mean Jeremy can come home now?" asked Iona.

"That will be a little more difficult now that the legal wheels of justice have rolled against Jeremy. First, we must plead with the crown attorney to dismiss all charges against Michael. This may then have to go through the judge to agree to dismiss all charges through a preliminary hearing. We have already set a court date. The fiasco has now become a very complex legal nightmare. It may take weeks or months to get him totally exonerated."

After they released Iona from the hospital, Michael drove her home. She sighed a great sigh of relief as she entered her house, knowing it was just a matter of time before they returned to their former life. She called Jeremy on the satellite phone and told him about everything that had happened in the past few hours.

"You risked your life for me," said Jeremy.

"Well, now, we are even." laughed Iona.

"I think we still have an uphill battle, though," said Jeremy.

He told Iona about Brian and Julie's findings of unusual activity on Leaf Cay in the Bahamas and how this could be where Julian was hiding. He also said that he did not think Julian would stop searching for him. Julian would continue to try to kill him until Jeremy stopped him.

"Julian believes that I am the biggest threat to his new life. He has the power and resources to stop me, so I will have to stop him first. It doesn't sound like I'll be able to get a new passport until I am totally exonerated, so there is nowhere for me to go but to stay here for now."

"I'm catching the next flight to Samana. I miss you," said Iona. "I'll see you in a few days."

Chapter 32

Julie and Brian sat in their administrative office in the Georgetown clinic.

"We are not a lot further ahead," said Julie. "We saw something ominous going on with Leaf Cay, but we don't know if we can relate it to Jeremy."

"Jeremy's situation has improved over the last week," said Brian. "He will get the new passport once they have totally exonerated him. It may take a few more weeks for that to happen. Jeremy is concerned that Julian will try to silence him because of everything he learned about his drug production. Jeremy seems convinced that his only hope for survival is to get to Julian first. I don't think that Jeremy understands what he's getting himself into. Thanks to our criminal father, you and I have lived in the undercover world of illegal drugs all our lives. If Jeremy is truly hell-bent on jumping into this dangerous world, we must help him."

"Iona and I have talked to him," said Julie. "We tried to convince him it's not worthwhile and he should just return to Toronto and pick up his life. His answer to that is that he would be dead within 48 hours. He believes the drug culture is much more pervasive in the hospital than anyone except him has discovered."

Brian's phone rang. "I better get this." He said to Julie.

"Hello," said Brian. "Jose, let me put you on speaker. I'm here with my sister."

"Hi Julie," said Jose on the other end of the line. "I was told not to talk to anybody, but there is something weird going on with Leaf Cay. They have hired me to help manage the construction of the villa. They seem to want it to be built in a hurry. There are over 40 construction workers on the island at a time. The weird thing is they have at least 10 guards carrying guns hovering over us. We give them our cell phones every morning to prevent us from taking pictures. They said if we got caught talking to anybody about this construction, we would regret it, as would our families.

"The owner comes by occasionally. He is a short chubby guy who's bald but has a beard. He wears huge sunglasses as if to hide his face. Very weird. It looks like he is staying in the small cabin on the beach, but he's always surrounded by 10 guards."

"I know you need the money, Jose, but it sounds like a dangerous place. Just be careful. I appreciate you calling us. The life of one of our friends may be in danger, possibly because of what is going on there. When do you think you will complete the construction?" asked Brian.

"I predict completion in about two months," said Jose.

"Can you get us a copy of the construction plans from the head office?" asked Brian.

"No problem," said Jose. "I'm in the head office at least once a week to update them about the construction. I have access to the digital plans and will e-mail them to you in a few hours."

"Please, just be careful, Jose," pleaded Julie.

Julie and Brian looked at each other after the phone call finished. They always advocated for a drug-free Bahamas but appreciated that they fought a losing battle. Whenever they faced drug trafficking or any other dark situations, they had to get involved. They both moved carefully and tried to keep an arm's distance from danger. They did not trust the police force or the politicians. The only people they trusted were the Americans. Often, they left messages for the DEA or the United States Coast Guard. They were always careful not to identify themselves, as this was a very dangerous world in which they lived.

It was late afternoon, and Brian and Julie headed to Jackie's Fish Fry on Georgetown Wharf for dinner. They met some friends to have a few beers and eat fried fish after work. They lined up as they loaded the fried fish, rice, and corn on their plates. The TV blared over the bar. Brian laughed at a story that Julie finished telling their friends about a small boy in the clinic. He lost his toy pooch somewhere. The small boy ran into the operating room in the middle of an operation, completely naked before someone caught him. Brian glanced up at the TV and caught a picture of his friend Jose.

"An unknown assailant shot and killed Jose De Silva in broad daylight this afternoon as he sat having a drink at Staniel Cay Yacht Club. Anyone having information about this crime, please call 268-555-9111." Brian dropped his plate, and the food splattered everywhere.

"Oh my God," cried Brian in disbelief. "They killed Jose!"

Julie's eyes filled with tears. "I don't believe it," she said. "We were just talking with him this afternoon."

Brian and Julie looked at each other. They glanced around the Fish Fry restaurant. A few guests were in the outdoor restaurant, but no one seemed threatening. Their friends just sat down at an empty table, oblivious to what happened on the TV and were eating their dinner. "I hope that Jeremy and Iona are not in any trouble." They both ran out to the end of the pier to have privacy. They dialed the satellite phone number. There was no answer.

Chapter 33

The wind filled the sails as ***Iona, Too,*** smoothly sliced through the warm Caribbean Sea. The wind came from the north and blew them on a beam to reach their destination. They had been at sea for 2 days. Iona lay on the cushions in her bikini at the front of the boat in the warm sunshine as the wind gently blew her hair to the side. It had been a hectic couple of weeks.

10 days earlier, Michael expedited the dismissal of Jeremy's charges, and he now had received a complete pardon. It took about three days to get his passport Fed Ex'd to the Canadian embassy in Santo Domingo. Jeremy made a call to Pat Stirling of Embassy Yachts in Toronto.

Pat Stirling had been in the yacht brokering business for 30 years and was the Hanse dealer in Toronto. A few years earlier, Pat sold Jeremy Young his previous sailboat, a Hanse 508. Pat Stirling followed Jeremy Young's dramatic story in the news. The sinking of a boat as beautiful as a Hanse in the middle of the ocean by ruthless drug pirates devastated Pat. He was sitting in his office when his phone vibrated. The screen read, "Unknown number."

"Hello Pat, this is Jeremy."

The shock of hearing Jeremy's voice caused a momentary loss of words for Pat. Losing a sailboat in his world was one of life's most devastating events, on par with losing a loved one. He could only imagine Jeremy's trauma, and it wasn't easy to know what to say. Pass on condolences about the loss of the sailboat. Congratulate him on his dismissal of the charges against him. Ask him how bad things really were.

"Hello?" asked Jeremy.

"Sorry, Jeremy," said Pat. "Not sure what to say after everything you have been through, but hearing your voice is good. How are you?"

"I am doing much better," said Jeremy. "The insurance company came through with the claim. I want to talk to you about getting a new boat. I've been looking at the new Hanse 510. What's the chance of getting one of those? I'm in the Dominican Republic, so the best thing for me would be to find a boat somewhere in the Caribbean."

"Let me check into it, and I'll get back to you," said Pat. Jeremy gave Pat his satellite phone number and hung up after a few more pleasantries.

Within 2 hours, Pat called Jeremy on his satellite phone.

"I found a beauty. It's in Puerto Rico. The owner backed out of the deal at the last minute after delivering the boat, so they were looking for a new buyer. The good news is that the amount of the insurance payout will cover the cost of the new model," said Pat as Jeremy and Iona listened to the speaker. "You do not have to pay the 13% duty nor the 10% new Canadian luxury tax. That almost covers the 25% increased production costs of the new sailboat. The only downside is that you cannot bring the boat back into Canada unless, at some point, you pay these taxes. You should be fine if you keep the boat in the Caribbean."

Jeremy and Iona readily agreed to the purchase. They transferred the funds to Pat electronically. The transfer of ownership happened within two days. They would register the boat in Puerto Rico. Iona and Jeremy could pick it up within a week.

In another unexpected development, the reverend had really fallen for Iona. Embedded in his drug-crazed brain, the signals that Iona had imprinted were as powerful as his craving for the cocaine/remifentanil drug. Dr. Rick Mandel had harnessed the drug craving, but nothing would tame his desire for Iona. Hearing her voice would give him at least a little relief. Although Michael was not in favor, the reverend insisted on speaking to Iona to apologize for his abysmal behavior during the assault. He also had some information but would only give it to Iona. Reluctantly, Iona complied. She listened to his weepy apologies and drug-related explanations for his inappropriate behavior.

After listening to his nonsensical rambling for ten minutes,

Iona said. "Reverend, what you did to me was awful. However, I was not totally honest with you either. If this makes us even, then I forgive you."

The reverend went silent for ten seconds. "You do not know how much that means to me," he said. "There is something else. I am feeling bad about everything. The treatment of Jeremy was abysmal. My lawyer says the more I cooperate, the less time I'll spend in jail. I wanted to tell you about a name that Julian kept on mentioning. John Papadopoulos. He is in Falmouth Harbor in Antigua. I do not have all the details, but I know he is the one that Julian used to get his new identity."

Iona was silent on the other end of the line. The call was on the speakerphone so that Jeremy could also hear every word. She quietly hung up the phone without saying goodbye. Iona had been with Jeremy at the Eco Lodge for the last 4 weeks. This was unexpected information. Jeremy did a Google search and discovered that John Papadopoulos had a mega-yacht for rent. His home address was at the Antigua Yacht Club.

That was where they were heading in their new sailboat. It would take another day of smooth sailing to get there. Iona felt happy and safe for the first time in many months. She glanced up at Jeremy, who adjusted the boat's course using the auto helm. They just passed the British Virgin Islands and were now on a course sailing south of St. Martin. Jeremy trimmed the sails perfectly, adjusted for the change in wind direction, and the sailboat responded. Iona basked in the wind's power as the sailboat gently drove through the swells. She drifted off to a restful sleep with the peaceful rocking of the seas.

Chapter 34

Julie and Brian motored up the mangrove-lined river on their way to the Eco Lodge. They flew to Samana airport in their Piper Cherokee with their pilot, Hector. The flight took 4 hours. They crossed Samana Bay in a speedboat and were now in a small inflatable dinghy, almost there. The call to the satellite phone went unanswered. Calls to the staff at the Eco Lodge resulted in no answer. They were worried that something terrible had happened.

They tied the inflatable to the dinghy dock and hiked the last two kilometers to the Eco Lodge. The lodge was in shambles. The restaurant had bullet holes in some tables and chairs. They climbed the stairs to the presidential suite, where Iona and Jeremy stayed. They knocked on the door, but the door swung open on its own. Someone tore the place upside down. They had smashed the satellite phone on the floor, and the pieces lay everywhere. The beds were upside down, and a broken window led out to the balcony.

Julie and Brian went down to the staff quarters, and all the doors were open. The place was empty. There was no one there. It looked like they left in a hurry because some half-eaten food was still on the table, with some of the coffee cups half filled. They descended the stairs to the main lobby of the Eco Lodge, although they expected it would be empty because there had been no guests. They had ripped the phones from the desk, leaving the cables hanging from the wall. The place was completely empty.

Julie and Brian then made their way through the jungle along a small, well-traveled path to the tiny village where many of the employees lived. As they walked to the village, a young villager jumped in front of them with a machete. He said in Spanish, "Get out of here! You're not welcome!".

"Phillipe," said Brian. "Is that you?" Brian recognized him from his frequent visits to the village. He was the grandson of the chief cook, Rachel.

"Oh my God," exclaimed Phillipe, "It's you and Julie. I thought it was them coming back for us."

"What happened?" asked Brian.

"Let's talk with my grandmother. She was there when everything happened," said Phillipe.

They walked down the path further to a small brick house. Rachel greeted them with hugs and kisses. Rachel was in her 60s but as fit as someone in their 40s. As the family's matriarch and chief cook, she managed the Eco Lodge like it was hers. Her treatment of them was like they were her own kids. She remembered their birthdays and threw a gigantic party for them on those special days. She told them frequently that she loved them. This was the closest thing to family that these two had ever experienced.

"They came in the evening 3 days ago," said Rachel. "There were about twenty of them. We saw them come up the mangrove river carrying guns and wearing camouflage, so we recognized they were trouble. We had time to round everybody up, including Jeremy and Iona, and hid in the caves. They could never find us there. By the time they left, it was dark, but we were worried they would return. I am so sorry we didn't take better care of your friends."

"Rachel, what do you mean? You saved their lives. Once again, you have taken care of everyone. Thank you! Any idea who they were or where they were from?" asked Julie.

"We could hear them talking through the walls of the caves, and they were speaking English." Said Rachel. "From how they talked, Jeremy and Iona said they were looking for them. After they left, we were afraid to return to the Eco Lodge in case those wicked men came back looking for them, so we have been hiding here in the village. My husband drove Iona and Jeremy to Santo Domingo airport, and they caught an evening flight to San Juan in Puerto Rico 3 days ago. We have not heard from them since."

Rachel's narrative had Brian and Julie hanging on every word. They had spoken with Iona and Jeremy about a week prior, so they knew about their new sailboat. They planned to stay at the Eco Lodge while the boat was being commissioned. Jeremy and Iona were on the run, hiding from Julian's long reach. Now, Brian agreed with Jeremy. Julian needed to be stopped.

Chapter 35

John Papadopoulos was sitting at the bar in his usual spot at the Antigua Yacht Club. He was drunk. He always imagined that once he achieved a certain amount of wealth, he would also achieve happiness and contentment. Instead, he was bored. A family from the United Emirates rented his mega yacht for the next two weeks, so he was stuck in the Antigua Yacht Club Marina hotel. There was nothing for him to do but lines of cocaine and alcohol. He realized he had no purpose or goals in his life. To live happily ever after, he needed to de-program his brain. Cocaine and rum had been the best antidote, but they were no longer effective in achieving happiness. He suffered from severe anxiety and restlessness. His past shady money-making schemes made him hesitant to travel too far from Antigua, like Greece. He moved to Antigua 3 years ago and, so far, had avoided detection from those that looked for him. He was not keen to risk this life he made for himself.

John grew up in Athens, Greece. He was the only son of a shopkeeper. His parents gave him an excellent education. He attended the Athens University of Economics and Business. His first job was as a junior investment advisor at the National Bank of Greece. He was so bored that often he would not come to work. Making lots of money was his dream, but he wasn't willing to put in any effort. By using other people's money, he believed he could generate the most income. He used wealthy clients' accounts to trade in the stock market. He did well and accumulated about $100,000 in his personal account. Nobody was wise to his scheme until the 2008 crash. The value of the stocks plummeted by half, and suddenly, he was $1,000,000 short. It did not take long for the bank to notice the strange transactions, and they fired John. The only reason they did not take legal action against John was to preserve the bank's reputation.

John was out of work, but he found he could log into travelers' laptops if he hung around the airport while they used the free Wi-Fi. He took their visa card information, driver's license information, and passport information if he was very lucky. At first, he just used the Visa information to buy things to resell on Kijiji. He soon realized that he could tap into a market where, if someone wanted to change their identity, he could sell that information. One of his unsuspecting victims suddenly suffered a heart attack and cardiac arrest. The traveler was trying to book a flight on his laptop while in the AmEx lounge. He died in the emergency clinic at the airport, but not before John downloaded the information on his computer. He sold that identity for $50,000 to an Irish man wishing to avoid paying alimony to his wife of 30 years.

That was the beginning of his new identity business. When he found out about immigrants that died on their way to Europe on boats that sank, he gathered their names and information. A small boy washed up on the shores of a Greek island after the boat capsized and he drowned. John had that boy still alive with an adopted by a couple in Montreal. That boy had grown up now, had a social insurance number and paid taxes. John had that legitimate Canadian passport in his files, hidden on his mega yacht. Although that boy would now be about 10 years younger than him, he didn't think anyone would notice. He saved that identity for himself.

When the tax department audited him, he fled Greece. The tax department tracked him for about three years. They wanted to understand how he lived in a $1,000,000 home overlooking the ocean and how he drove a Porsche Cayenne if he had no income. Rather than go through a costly legal battle, which he would likely lose, he changed his identity to John Papadopoulos. John was an expatriated Greek who planned on living part-time in Antigua. He had stolen his identity information a few years earlier at Athens International Airport. Having the real John Papadopoulos disappear while on a fishing trip, 10 miles off Jolly Harbour in Antigua costs little. With no physical body to prove death with certainty, stealing the identity was a straightforward task.

So now, a few years into his new identity, John Papadopoulos was bored. He scanned around the bar, and it was the same boring crowd that kept on coming. Most British patrons worked on the enormous yachts as captains, engineers, maintenance crew, hostesses, and cooks. After a while, they all had the same stories. They searched for a life of adventure and action on the ocean. Many believed they did not fit into a normal society. Some women hoped to find a well-to-do benefactor on the large yachts but soon realized that men were the same everywhere. Mostly, men were pigs.

A handsome couple walked in and sat on the bar stools beside him. They ordered two rum punches and quietly chatted with each other. After finishing his drink, the man stood up and said to the woman, "I'll be back in a few hours."

John stared at the woman. She was beautiful. This could be the most excitement he had in the past week. He had a few hours to make his move before the man would come back. John sidled over to the empty barstool next to the woman. The conversation started with the usual pleasantries and introductions. Before long, John knew he had this amazing creature under his thumb. She stared into his eyes, laughed at his silly jokes, and touched his arm, allowing the fingers to linger too long. An hour passed, and he invited her to his room for a drink. To his surprise, she readily agreed.

They laughed at something she said as he unlocked his door and entered his hotel room. After shutting the door, he closed the safety lock. He turned on the lights. He stopped dead in his tracks. The man who had entered the bar with the woman was sitting on the chair beside the bed. John's laptop computer was open on the small table beside the chair.

"Is this a shakedown?" asked John angrily. "Because if it is, you will never get away with it. I am well known around here, and the police will track you down."

"I'm going to ask you once," said Jeremy. "I would like you to tell me the identity you gave Julian Yakoby and where he is hiding."

"I have no clue what you're referring to," said John.

Jeremy stood up from the chair, saying nothing. He walked up to John and punched him in the face. John went rolling on the floor. He was unconscious.

Chapter 36

When John Papadopolous woke up, he quickly discerned he was somewhere at sea on a boat. There was no land in sight. His initial thought was that he was on his mega yacht, but there seemed to be too much movement for the large boat. He realized he was on a smaller boat. He could not move. They tied him onto a chair on the swim platform at the back of a boat. The sun shone brightly, and the wind was mild. The boat did not move through the water but rocked gently with the small waves on the open ocean. His face hurt, and he remembered getting punched by a man who waited in his room for him. There was a beautiful woman totally enamored by him, he remembered.

Jeremy and Iona hopped down on the swim platform. "John Papadopoulos," said Jeremy. "Three years ago, he went on a fishing trip near Jolly Harbor, never to be seen again."

"It's a common name in Greece," said John. "Clearly, more than one of us with the same name."

Iona said, "John Papadopoulos was 63 years old when he disappeared. You are no older than 48. I doubt you will get much support from the local police force if you complain about us. In fact, the only thing you will do if you ever get away from us is to disappear somewhere else."

"We only want information on one individual," said Jeremy. "And then we'll let you go."

Iona said. "We want to know about Julian Yacoby's new identity and where he is."

"I haven't the faintest clue what you're saying," said John. John suddenly knew who these people were. They were Jeremy and Iona. These were the two people that Julian had already tried to kill by throwing them off their boat, hoping no one would ever see them again. Somehow, they also escaped and survived the botched attempt to kill them at the Eco Lodge. Julian warned him they were problematic and needed to be eliminated.

John studied them intently, knowing that they were not killers. He was certain they would not hurt him. They were both doctors and law-abiding citizens. As far as he was aware, neither had any weapons training nor training in fighting. He was certain they had led privileged lives and did not know what they were up against dealing with Julian and him. He dealt with many like them through his business of selling stolen identities. Most of those seeking new identities were in the same socio-economic category as them. Manipulating them came easily to John. He was a master at this art of deception. John remained confident that he had the advantage over them because he lived with a different code of moral values. The only moral code he followed centered on how he could best benefit.

John was sitting on a chair balanced at the stern of the boat on the swim platform. They positioned the chair so it faced the bow of the boat. The swimming deck was almost 2 feet lower than the cockpit floor, and they fixed his hands with zip ties to the railing. The arms rested on the floor of the cockpit. He watched as Jeremy unrolled his bag of instruments. There was disinfectant, bandages, scalpels, syringes and needles, sutures, and many other surgical instruments. Jeremy arranged them on the cockpit floor in front of John.

"Here's how it will work for you, John Papadopoulos," said Jeremy. "I'm going to ask you again. If you don't give me the answer I am looking for, I'm going to cut off the small finger of your right hand. I will then ask you a second time, and if you don't give me the answer I need, I will cut off the fourth finger of your right hand. I will continue to cut off all your fingers until none is left in either hand."

John could tell that Jeremy was bluffing. It was obvious to John that Jeremy was uncomfortable in threatening to do such a mutilating act on a fellow human being. John recognized that this was not something a typical person, let alone a medical professional would even entertain. John was an expert in reading people, which is why he succeeded. Besides, Iona, his wife, was standing next to him. She would never let him do such a thing.

"What is the identity of Julian, and where is he hiding?" asked Jeremy.

"I have no clue what you are referring to," said John with a confident smile.

With lightning speed, Jeremy pulled out the scalpel and sliced off the small finger of John's right hand. He positioned the scalpel so it severed the cartilage and tendons just below where the finger joined the palm of the hand. Jeremy finished the entire process in less than 3 seconds. Blood is pumped from the severed digital arteries over the cockpit floor, spewing an arch of blood from the base of the severed digit.

John's first reaction was disbelief. There was a moment of silence before he let out a bloodcurdling scream. He stared down at his severed finger, now lying on the cockpit floor. Blood spewed at an incredible rate from the base of the stump. The pain was the worst pain that John had ever felt. He kept on screaming and could not stop. He wriggled his wrist, trying to get free, but they fixed the wrists in position with the zip ties. The zip ties cut into his wrist, causing more bleeding and pain. He watched as Jeremy controlled the bleeding from the digital arteries with surgical instruments. The bleeding stopped. The pain continued. The screaming continued. Jeremy and Iona remained silent as Jeremy sutured the digital arteries and then closed the skin over the top of where the fifth finger had been. Jeremy picked up the severed digit and threw it into the water.

John hyperventilated and heard his heart pounding in his chest quickly. He felt lightheaded. He thought he was going to pass out. The pain was so severe; he could not stop crying. Tears ran down his face as he kept screaming. After a period, the screaming settled down to a whimper. Now he was sobbing, attempting to comprehend what had occurred. He had totally misread those two. He could not believe what had happened.

John sat bound in the chair at the sailboat's stern, unable to cease crying. Nothing like this had ever happened to him before. John and Iona descended into the main salon of the sailboat, so he was by himself. He recognized he was in no position to negotiate or even predict what they would do next. He also understood that he could not go to the police even after the mutilation; it was too risky. They might identify him as an impostor.

Jeremy and Iona ascended the companionway from the main salon and approached John. Before they could say anything, John started talking. He shared all about his past; he told them what he knew about the drug production facility; he told them how Julian approached him to get a new identity; he revealed to them about buying Leaf Cay; and he informed them all about Andy Smith,

Julian's new identity. Julian's banking information that he had secretly stolen, he shared with Jeremy. John talked for about 2 hours. John went on and on, and Jeremy and Iona listened intently, jotting down some notes.

Jeremy once more descended into the main salon and returned with John's laptop computer. "I want all Julian's bank accounts, including his numbered Panamanian accounts and how I can access them. I need you to download everything onto this USB."

John's fingers could not stop trembling, so Jeremy had to punch most of the keys. The amount of cash that Julian stashed away caused Jeremy's eyes to open widely. In the various bank accounts and numbered companies, there must be over $3 billion. That he could accumulate this wealth without detection in this day of electronic oversight staggered Jeremy. All governments were monitoring illegal drug operations. Jeremy surmised that the only way Julian got away with this was by knowing who to bribe. John also provided that list. Included were the amounts paid to individual bankers, officials, police, and politicians. The list was long. The information was damaging and dangerous. Jeremy was sure that many on the list would kill to prevent this information from getting into the hands of honest authorities. John explained how he had completed the transactions covertly to avoid suspicion. The system was foolproof until today. After they completed the download, Jeremy heaved the laptop into the Caribbean Sea.

After John stopped talking, they released his zip ties. They had broken John. He quietly sat in the cockpit and stared at his hand. He said nothing. Jeremy and Iona sailed the boat back to Falmouth harbor. After anchoring in the harbor, they dropped their dinghy into the water. Iona, Jeremy, and John tentatively boarded the dinghy. The three motored to the Antigua Yacht Club and dropped John off at the dock. The last John saw of them, ***Iona Too,*** was sailing out of Falmouth harbor. John fervently wished that he would never encounter them again.

Chapter 37

The wind blew 15 knots off the beam. The conditions made for perfect sailing. ***Iona Too*** flew along at around 9 knots in the gentle seas. The sun shone brightly in a cloudless sky. Jeremy steered at the helm. Iona lay on the cushions at the bow of the boat, resting with the gentle sway of the boat. Jeremy estimated they were about 30 miles from St. Barts. They sailed past the island of Monserrat. The volcano, still active, spewed gray ash into the clouds. It was magnificent to see. They headed for Anse de Colombier in St. Barts. They planned to anchor for the evening, clear out early, and head for St. Martin.

It had been an emotionally taxing 24 hours. The actions taken against John Papadopoulos by Jeremy and Iona were not characteristic of them. When they planned to get information from him, they had not completely worked out how they would do it. First, tricking him into leaving the bar with Iona was the deception expected from psychopaths. However, they justified this part to themselves. To interact in a fair competition with psychopaths, they had to think and act like them. Jeremy appreciated if he was to threaten to cut off John's finger, he must be prepared to do it. Iona and Jeremy discussed how this mutilating, heinous act might affect them. They balanced the risk of John reporting them to the authorities and decided this would not happen. The biggest risk was how they coped with the guilt and shame of doing such a terrible thing to another human being.

What made it easier for Jeremy was the smug attitude of John Papadopoulos. The way he sat in the chair almost dared him to do such a thing, believing that it was completely against Jeremy's nature. That John had gotten away with such horrendous criminal activities, such as the murder of the real John Papadopoulos, sickened Jeremy. The lack of accountability infuriated Jeremy. Jeremy took responsibility for that terrible attack on the Eco Lodge directed against him by Julian. He had to protect those lovely families that worked there for all those years. He experienced no guilt for the injuries he inflicted on the reverend and his co-worker. It surprised Jeremy that he had no guilt about chopping off John's finger. The stark change in his behavior contrasted with the drive to "do the right thing" in his former life. Jeremy hoped he was not turning into the monster he was trying to slay.

Jeremy and Iona arrived at Anse de Colombier in St. Barts just as it was getting dark. They heard from other cruisers that checking in with the authorities was unnecessary if they planned to stay overnight. About 20 other boats anchored there, rocking slightly in the gentle swells from the North Atlantic. They found a protected spot away from other boats, which shielded them from the easterly winds. They dropped their anchor in the clear water, ensuring it held in the soft sand. Other cruisers approaching them were unexpected. Having turned off their AIS, they were invisible to other cruisers. They kept track of the cruiser's social media posts and WhatsApp posts. If any cruisers were curious about them, they would deflect by posting false information. Sometimes they might identify themselves from Denmark, having just sailed across the Atlantic from Cape Verde. Other times they would identify as American, heading for Grenada for hurricane season.

Jeremy and Iona were emotionally and physically exhausted. They had not slept for the last 36 hours. After a meal of reheated spaghetti and meatballs, they fell into a profound sleep for the next 12 hours. They woke up at 7 in the morning feeling rested.

Iona raised the anchor using the windlass while Jeremy steered the boat. Slipping out of the protected harbor, they headed towards St. Martin. They needed to provision the sailboat as they were running low on food. They had a water maker, so there was no shortage of fresh water.

Jeremy and Iona cautiously ventured beneath the drawbridge into the Simpson Bay Lagoon. They secured a mooring on the French side, away from the other boats. Jeremy and Iona launched their dinghy and checked in with French customs and immigration with no difficulty. They spent the rest of the day provisioning food from the best French grocery stores.

Jeremy and Iona were sitting on the veranda of La Cigale

restaurant overlooking Simpson's Bay Lagoon. Witnessing the sun setting over their boat was magnificent. They just finished dinner, and both agreed it was the best French cuisine they had ever experienced. They were drinking their cappuccinos, admiring the view, when a familiar voice bellowed, "Jeremy! What in the devil's name are you doing here?"

It was Robert Planter, the chief of psychiatry at Jeremy's hospital. "What an incredible coincidence," he exclaimed. "You would be the last person on earth I would expect to run into in this fancy French restaurant in St. Martin, of all places, after everything you've been through. I apologize for how things worked out, and I take full responsibility for treating you terribly in the hospital. I was totally wrong about Julian. I understand now how he is so dangerous. His mental condition is unstable. I am sorry that I was not more supportive of you. I feel bad."

Jeremy and Iona viewed Robert skeptically. They had no intention of accepting his claim that this was a coincidence. During their entire trip, they were always on guard to run into people that recognized them, understanding that they could trust no one from the hospital. They disabled their AIS and disguised the name *Iona Too* to make it more difficult to be identified. They suspected that someone had tracked them.

"We flew in a few days ago and are staying at Le Martin

Boutique Hotel for a few more days," lied Jeremy. We needed some restful time to reassemble after all that had occurred.

"No kidding," said Robert. "One of our big donors offered my wife and me the use of their 110-foot mega yacht. There are 6 crew looking after the two of us. Let's meet for dinner on board tomorrow night. I anchored us in Marigot Bay just outside the lagoon."

"Sounds great!" said Jeremy, going with the flow of conversation.

"I'll ask the crew to pick you up at the launch at your hotel, say 7:00 PM? I'll have you back in the hotel by midnight," said Robert excitedly.

After exchanging farewells, Iona and Jeremy remained in the restaurant for another 1/2 hour. Wanting to make sure that nobody was following them, they walked along Voorstraat, popping in and out of stores. They found one with a back entrance and exited that way. They followed the shoreline back to the restaurant and to the dinghy dock. Because it was so late, few people were walking around. It was unlikely Robert Planter or one of his hired crew had followed them. They powered up the dinghy's engine and journeyed back to their sailboat.

Jeremy and Iona were the first ones under the drawbridge exiting the lagoon in the morning. The night before, they went through French customs online. They changed their original plans. They originally planned to island hop all the way to the Bahamas. The plan was to stop at The British Virgin Islands, The Spanish Virgin Islands, Puerto Rico, and the Dominican Republic. Knowing Robert would reveal their location after meeting with him, and they chose to sail to the Dominican Republic. The trip would take approximately three days.

With two of them on board, they agreed it was important to always have someone on deck to keep an eye out for other boats. Their AIS was turned off to avoid being tracked. They had the radar activated so they could observe any boat traffic. They did three-hour shifts. When Jeremy was on shift, Iona would rest, and then they would change shifts. Sometimes that meant they slept in the cockpit, other times in the aft cabin, which was less bouncy. The winds were favorable for a run to the Dominican Republic, coming from the northeast at around 15 knots. It was Caribbean sailing at its best in the constant warm easterly trade wind breeze. There was peace and contentment while staring at the stars at night. Life was simple on the water. If only it could go on like this forever.

Chapter 38

After anchoring *Iona Too* in Los Haitises National Park, Dominican Republic, Jeremy and Iona traveled to the Eco Lodge. They reunited with Julie and Brian at the Eco Lodge. Jeremy and Iona arrived after three days of sailing from St. Martin. Brian and Julie flew in from Georgetown to Samana and then, by speedboat, across the Bay of Samana.

Brian and Julie excitedly hugged Iona and Jeremy, squeezing them so tightly that they could hardly breathe. "It's so great to see you!" cried Julie.

"You two have been our lifesavers," said Iona. She was crying and couldn't stop the tears. She was so happy to see them.

"It's true," said Jeremy. "Without you, we would have been killed by now. We'll never be able to repay you for all you have done for us."

"I'd like you to meet Commander Bennett from The Commando Squadron," said Brian. "We went to school together and have been friends forever. Commander Bennett will teach us hand-to-hand combat and weapon use. We may need it if we get stuck in a difficult situation with Julian."

George Bennett was 18 when he entered the Military in the Bahamas. The Bahamas, surrounded by water, has a tiny military composed mainly of a naval force. Commander Bennett's values were identical to those of the Royal Bahamas Defence Force. The values he swore to uphold included protecting the integrity of the Bahamas, a country he loved; to, help those in need following hurricanes or other disasters, to patrol its waters; but for him, the most important value was to protect the islands from drugs. This defined his life's mission. George was the commander of the elite commando squadron. George Bennett trained with the American special forces, and his major role was to serve as the main Drug Enforcement branch of the squadron. Billions of dollars of cocaine passed through the Bahamas yearly, and he was determined to eliminate the flow. He no longer trusted his fellow commandos. The lucrative offers from drug cartels diverted their special hand-to-hand combat and weaponry training to the drug lords. They hired many of his best-trained commandos.

George's father had been killed by Brian and Julie's father. They established the Royal Bahamas Defence Force in the early 1980s. George's father joined the military and patrolled waters off of Norman Cay. It was a bright sunny day with a very light wind coming from the east. The sun was in his eyes, and even though he wore sunglasses, it wasn't easy to see. A plane was coming to land at Norman's Cay. They knew this was a huge part of the drug operation, and many planes had landed and refueled on their way to Miami to distribute drugs. Because of the enormous quantities of money involved, most authorities would look the other way, but not George's father.

The plane appeared to land on the runway, but it seemed too fast. It looked like the plane was practicing a "touch and go" maneuver and trying to gain some elevation when the left propeller struck the tarmac. The plane barreled along the runway and over the edge of the island. It flipped over into the lagoon. George's father immediately sprang into action to help. He revved up the engine of the military launch and raced to where the plane went into the water. Two people were floating in the water who were uninjured. They were both drunk. He pulled them out of the water and into his boat. Another boat coming from Norman Cay approached him. He recognized the driver as Brian's father. They had grown up together.

George's father announced he would arrest the two men for drunk and disorderly conduct while flying an airplane. Brian's father pulled out his gun and shot him in the head. George's father died instantly. They kept the incident hidden from public view and only disclosed it after they shut the Norman key drug operation down in the 1980s. Some criminals willingly shared this story and similar stories for a lighter sentence in jail. It was only because of corruption at top levels that kept Brian's father from being charged with murder.

George Bennett was now 43 years old but had the body of

a 22-year-old. He had less than 5% body fat and kept extremely fit. The best trained him, and now he was in charge of the commando squadron of the Royal Bahamas Defence Force. He trained others to be quick and skilled in hand-to-hand combat and weaponry. Brian and George developed a solid bond because of their common goal of ridding the Bahamas of drugs and the corruption that goes along with it. They acknowledged they were fighting a losing battle. They did not trust the police, military, or politicians, and they had difficulty finding others that would risk their lives to help. By helping Jeremy and Iona bring down Julian, they would prevent yet another drug operation from developing in the Bahamas on Leaf Cay.

The Eco Lodge returned to normal activity. Rachel, the chief cook and manager, cleaned up all the mess made by the attack. The grounds looked beautiful. There were flowers and mango trees with ripe mangoes hanging from the branches. About 20 workers in the lodge groomed the property and kept things in order. Rachel was ecstatic that Brian and Julie would stay with them for the next two weeks. She did not know exactly what they were up to but learned over the years not to ask too many questions. For 30 years, the Eco Lodge has supported her and twenty other families in the village. The attack had threatened her livelihood and family. She felt much safer now that Julie and Brian stayed at the Eco Lodge.

For the next two weeks, Jeremy and Iona learned how to

defend themselves against attackers. They learned how to block a punch. Jeremy and Iona learned how to use the attacker's momentum against them to throw them off balance. They learned how to defend themselves against an attack with a knife. They learned how to disarm somebody carrying a gun at close quarters. Learning to avoid and release themselves from a neck hold made them feel safer. They learned how to make someone unconscious quickly and dislocate an attacker's shoulder to immobilize them.

Commander Bennett was keen to teach them how to shoot guns. Jeremy and Iona drew the line at this. There was no way they could fire a gun at anybody under any circumstance. They discussed this at length and realized they could not take someone's life. Their plan for Julian was to disable him, to prevent him from harming anyone else. That may involve destroying all his cocaine, bank accounts, and properties, so he had nowhere to go or live. They planned to deliver him to the authorities and let the law take care of him. They were uncertain how they would accomplish this, but they knew they could never kill another human being in cold blood by firing a gun at them.

After two intense weeks of training, they were ready to move on to the next step.

Chapter 39

Michael sat at his desk in his law office in a downtown Toronto high-rise tower. From the 46th floor, he had a magnificent view of Toronto harbor. He saw the sailboats on the lake. It was a beautiful sunny late spring afternoon. The sailboats out on the lake made him think of Jeremy and Iona. So much had happened in the past few months it was difficult to keep track of everything that had happened to them. It had been a rollercoaster ride for him as well. He had never experienced such a crazy file that was getting crazier all the time. The legal perspective of what he could do versus his moral perspective of what he needed to do to help Jeremy and Iona conflicted with him.

He spent the last two days reviewing the encrypted files of Julien's bank accounts Jeremy had sent him. Jeremy explained to him how he got the files. This was totally out of bounds from the legal perspective. For the law to function in a civilized world, it is all about process. That included getting information. If the way Jeremy got the files was flawed, they could not use the entire information in a court of law. Michael understood he could not use the information that Jeremy had illegally obtained by cutting off a man's finger. That is why it is so hard to catch criminals and put them in jail. The principles of law are based on fairness and natural justice. It was very frustrating for Michael to be in this position.

However, Michael believed in the principle that knowledge is power. Michael believed he might use this knowledge to leverage a conviction or plea bargaining, even if the legal system could not use these files. He was also bound by client privilege confidentiality. He was under strict directions from Jeremy not to share this information until directed.

His advice to Jeremy was to return to Toronto and let someone else deal with this underworld that was immune to the arms of the law. His advice was simple. Give the information to the police and let them deal with it. Jeremy had no business dealing with these criminals and was clearly out of his depth. He advised Jeremy that he could have his old life back in Toronto if he wished. Michael negotiated with the CEO and chief of staff at his hospital, and they agreed to continue to pay for his salary as chief of surgery, which was about $16,000 a month. He also promised to sue them for damages and said he would address this part later when the full extent of the damages had been determined.

Michael's cell phone rang. He was expecting a call from Jeremy. "How are you, Jeremy?"

Jeremy said, "Never better. I am sailing in a tropical paradise with a beautiful woman. The winds are fair, and I have following seas. At the moment, I do not have a worry in the world."

"Ha ha," said Michael. "I wish I could say the same. That

information you sent me is too hot to handle. We will find it challenging to use those files in court because they were obtained illegally. However, the information is provocative. My advice to you is to get back to Toronto as quickly as possible and get your life back. You are going to come to great harm dealing with these characters. We can discuss how to make that information public and get it to the proper authorities who can deal with it."

Michael explained how he had re-established Jeremy's chief of surgery salary. He described how Jeremy would get a settlement to cover the legal costs and other damages.

Jeremy said, "Michael, it's a different world on the ocean. I've had plenty of time to think about what life is all about. There is something very calming and special about being on the water. I have concluded that my life will never be the same, and I will never get my old life back.

"It is perhaps difficult for you to understand this, Michael because you believe so much in the legal system, but I have seen what Julian can do. He tried to kill me 3 times now. He will not stop trying. I also believe he will harm others I am close to, and I cannot let that happen. I learned a lot about psychopaths in the past few months. They differ from you and me. At some point, to fight them, it is necessary to think like them. I have traveled down that path. There is no turning back. Life will never be the same for me."

"What are you going to do?" asked Michael tentatively.

"I'm going to stop Julian," said Jeremy. "I'm not sure how, but I've never been more prepared than I am now. In the meantime, perhaps you could keep that information safe, and we can discuss further when I have a plan in motion."

They discussed a few other pleasantries before hanging up. Michael looked down at the boats in the Toronto harbor, gracefully moving through the water. With their colorful spinnakers launched, the view was spectacular from 46 floors above. The seas were so gentle in this civilized, protected part of the world. Yet not far away, recent events exposed Jeremy and Iona to stormy waters as they entered the shadowy world of drug dealers. The thought crossed his mind that there was a real possibility he would never see Jeremy alive again.

Chapter 40

When Derek Kwasme awoke, he was in a hospital. He lay flat on the hospital bed and had a nasogastric tube in his nose. They attached him to an intravenous and monitored his blood pressure, pulse, and respiratory rate. The surgeon from last night just walked into the room. Derek had pain in his abdomen from the incision, and the events of last night came back to him.

"How are you this morning?" asked the surgeon.

Derek stared at the surgeon. This was the man that had saved his life. "I'm OK," Derek whispered.

"He stabbed you in the abdomen. There was an injury to your small intestine, requiring resection of about 12 cm. from your small bowel. Fortunately, you have about 20 feet of small intestine left inside, so I don't think you'll even notice it's gone. Everything else was OK." said the surgeon.

"I'm Dr. Jeremy Young, the surgeon who operated on you last night. I expect you'll be here about four or five days, and then you'll be fit for discharge. What happened last night that got you stabbed?"

Derek felt relieved that someone was interested in speaking to him about what had happened. The emergency room doctor from last night had been dismissive and cynical. When the doctor asked,

Derek tried to explain he was not a drug dealer. Derek could tell that he did not believe him. He labeled him as another black kid with a drug problem. The surgeon seemed different. He seemed to care.

"I was walking home from the Baskin Robbins ice cream store on Jane and Finch," explained Derek. "One kid from school was doing a drug deal with one of my friends. I tried to stop it, and I got stabbed. The guy who stabbed me ran away."

Jeremy said, "You must tell your story to the police and identify the kid that stabbed you, so he won't do it again."

Derek said, "Not a good idea. They would only make trouble for my family. I need to find another way to stop these drug deals, which are bad for the neighborhood where I live."

Jeremy said, "Well, good luck then. Another thing I want to talk to you about is that after this kind of trauma, young men often have post-traumatic stress disorder, PTSD. If you want to talk with someone about that confidentially, here's a card for a psychotherapist. She is also my wife. I will send her a referral note if you ever decide to contact her."

Derek stared at the card after Jeremy left. Talking to someone about the occurrence wasn't necessary for him. The drug dealers were going to be dealt with according to his own plan. He was tough. He put the card in his wallet just in case.

A few months later, Derek woke up at night with nightmares. In his dream, someone broke into his home and stabbed him again. He was afraid to go to sleep. He could not concentrate at school and developed constant anxiety. Some days, he did not want to get out of bed. Sometimes, he cried for no reason. After a few weeks, he realized he had to do something. He thought about killing himself, but then he pulled out the card Jeremy had given him. He made an appointment to see Dr. Iona Young.

As soon as Derek walked into Iona's office, he knew he had made the right decision. The first session took about 1 1/2 hours. Derek outlined his symptoms following his stabbing. Iona described what would happen over the next few months and promised him he would see improvements quickly. She said she dealt with this kind of problem with many patients, with excellent results.

That was over four years ago. He remained indebted to Dr. Jeremy Young for saving his life. He was more indebted to Iona for helping him cope with the psychological damage following the trauma. Since then, he had become what others described as an IT geek. He hacked into the smartphones and emails of the unsophisticated drug dealers at his old school and shut down the payments and transfer of drugs. Although the drug dealing still happened, Derek made it much more difficult for them.

Derek moved on to more sophisticated drug dealers and their

bank accounts. He learned that the best way to damage drug operations was to send their money in different directions so they would blame each other. They already did not trust each other. If done correctly, they would try to destroy each other, trying to retrieve their cash.

When Iona and her lawyer Michael approached Derek to help destroy Julian, he knew exactly what to do. What made it especially easy was Iona and Jeremy had done all the hard work. They had given him all the banking information, the passwords, the bank accounts, and the two-step verification codes. All Derek had to do was re-direct the money. This saved him a lot of time. This was the damage to drug dealers he had been inflicting for the last few years. He was excited to work with Jeremy and Iona after everything they had done for him. "I'll make sure that no one will track who has done all this damage that I am about to cause to them. I will also install firewalls so that the process cannot be reversed once we start it," he had explained to Iona and Michael when they met.

Chapter 41

Jeremy and Iona left the Eco Lodge and Bay of Samana on a beautiful warm sunny Dominican Republic morning. The winds were from the east, so they motored into the wind until they cleared the Cape of Samana. From there, it was perfect sailing conditions to get to the Bahamas, which lay about 500 miles west. Completely naked in the cockpit, they lay basking in the warm sun. Periodically, one of them would drift off to sleep while the other would keep a watch for other boats. They had the radar on alert for boating activity, but few ships appeared on the radar screen as they were not near a major shipping channel.

Arriving in Georgetown, in the Bahamas, they anchored off Stocking Island among the hundreds of boats already there. The plan was to conceal their presence in plain sight. Hoping to avoid detection by Julian's rogues, they used a fake name, "*The Sailor*," to conceal the real name of their boat, "*Iona Too*." They took the dinghy across Elizabeth Harbor to Georgetown. They checked in with customs, and Brian and Julie met them at the Exuma dock.

"Come back to the house with us," said Julie. "We've got something to show you."

They hopped into Julie's Nissan Leaf and, within 10 minutes, arrived at their house in February Point. Julie made a traditional conch salad, and they each celebrated their reunion with a glass of white wine. Jeremy and Iona discussed their beautiful sailing trip from the Dominican Republic. It took 3 days. The weather was perfect, the trade winds were gentle, and the seas were fair. It was a relaxing and quiet time. There was plenty of time to plan and discuss their next steps.

While hunching over Brian's computer, Brian said, "Here are the plans for their villa, which is almost complete. They will move into the villa within the next two days. As you can tell, there are three floors and a large complex. There are cameras in every room. A command center is on the main floor at the back of the house. They have backup generators, so they are not totally dependent upon the power grid. They always have at least 20 guards on the property.

Commander Bennett has assembled 20 of his top trusted commandos for the mission. They practiced some dry run exercises, but none knew the plan was to go after this place on Leaf Cay. The only people appraised of the plan are the four of us and Commander Bennett. He will not inform his troops of the attack on the island until they're ready to land. This way, we will not alert Julian."

Jeremy said, "That sounds great. I will coordinate Julian's financial destruction at the same time as the attack on his property. Michael has been working with Derek Kwasme, our banking IT expert in Toronto. When the time comes, Iona, Julie, and Derek

Kwasme will electronically empty Julian's many bank accounts. They will distribute the money to various governments as taxes. Both governments of the Bahamas and Canada will get billions of dollars of unplanned extra tax revenue this year."

Julie said, "Commander Bennett and his team will apprehend Julian and lock him away in an undisclosed location so no one can reach him. We expect the extradition proceedings to go quickly, so he gets deported back to Canada to go through the legal system there. He will probably spend the rest of his life in prison. We will crash and burn the island so they cannot use it for drug distribution."

"Jeremy, are you sure you want to be part of the commando raid?" asked Brian. "It's going to be dangerous, and there's going to be guns, and we expect quite a battle."

"I have to be there, Brian," said Jeremy. "It is essential that Julian knows I am responsible for his downfall. That is the only way that I will feel safe. For a psychopath, he needs to understand that somebody smarter and more powerful defeated him. Otherwise, I will worry he will come after me. I will need to be looking over my shoulder for the rest of my life."

"Let's aim for 4 days from now," continued Jeremy. "That will give us time to get down to Staniel Cay and do a final survey before bringing him down. We need to ensure that everything is in place and that we have thought of every contingency."

Jeremy and Iona spent the night in the spare bedroom. In the morning, when they awoke, they went to the kitchen. Brian and Julie were drinking coffee and eating freshly baked croissants. They were confident about their plans and excited that things were moving along.

Brian motioned Jeremy to come out to the patio while Julie and Iona laughed at a story Iona was telling. Brian said, "It will not be safe for Iona for the next few days. I would suggest that she stay here with Julie."

Jeremy said, "I agree with you, Brian. I've discussed it with Iona, but she wants to come along. Maybe if you brought it up to her, she would listen."

There was a rustling in the hedge next to the patio. Brian turned around just as a large man leaped through the air and landed on Brian. He had a knife in his hand and jammed it to the hilt into his abdomen. Brian moaned softly, rolling his back with his hands around the knife in disbelief. Julie and Iona turned around at the sound of the commotion and screamed. The attacker looked up from the crouching position, then stood up and faced Jeremy. He pulled out a second knife from his belt.

Jeremy eyed the assailant calmly. He remained completely still, waiting for the assailant to make the first move. His pulse beat slowly. His breathing slowed down. Jeremy, accustomed to stressful, life-threatening situations during his career as a surgeon, assessed his options. He had trained himself to remain calm when the world was falling apart. The assailant seemed somewhat hesitant by this unusual calmness he saw with Jeremy. The reaction the assailant expected was terror.

Attempting to unnerve Jeremy, the assailant let out a loud war cry and charged forward with the knife, ready to slice into his abdomen. It was as if everything moved in slow motion for Jeremy. He waited until the assailant was within a few steps of him and then did the unexpected. Instead of backing away or moving right or left, Jeremy charged him. As the assailant tried to bring the knife forward, he was not quick enough. Jeremy brought his right hand up on the man's elbow and threw him off balance slightly, but enough to cause him to drop the knife. The assailant's momentum caused him to fly by Jeremy off balance. Jeremy brought his knee into the assailant's groin with such force that it caused him to flip over onto his back.

The assailant stood up somewhat unsteadily. He charged Jeremy with his hands outstretched, ready to grab him. Using his elbows, he forced the assailant's arms to fly above his head in one smooth move. Jeremy grabbed the man's hair and smashed the face onto his knee. He heard the bones of the face and nose crunch. The momentum of the off-balanced assailant focused all the forces onto the face, creating tremendous damage. The man lay on the patio unconscious, with blood pouring from his face. He appeared to be breathing irregularly and with a great deal of effort.

Although the entire attack had taken less than two minutes, Jeremy heard the sirens in the distance become louder as they approached the house. Jeremy turned to help his friend. Brian remained alert and awake despite his obvious injury and witnessed the entire attack. He was in great discomfort, and his hand held the knife to prevent it from moving.

Jeremy said, "It looks like Iona and Julie called for help, and the police and ambulance are coming. I will take care of you, as you are the only other general surgeon in the region."

Brian grimaced and said, "It hurts like hell, Jeremy."

The police ran to the back of the house and saw the carnage. A brief account of the events from Iona and Julie drew their attention to the unconscious man laying on the patio. He was oozing blood in several areas from his broken face. The hand of the man drifted to his face as he gained consciousness. He attempted to open his eyes. The eyes could not focus and looked in separate directions because of the severe facial injury. They slapped handcuffs on his wrists behind his back. They loaded him into the police cruiser.

The ambulance arrived within the next 60 seconds, and they eased Brian onto a gurney. Jeremy started a large-bore intravenous during the ambulance ride to the hospital. He pumped the saline solution intravenously. Brian was hypotensive and drifted in and out of consciousness during the 10-minute ride.

The small hospital had an adequate resuscitation room. Jeremy put a catheter into the bladder to measure the urine output, another large bore central line and a more intravenous saline solution. A family doctor stood by who also functioned as an anesthesiologist. He assisted with the resuscitation. Unfortunately, the small hospital had no blood bank, so a blood transfusion was not an option. Brian lost a lot of blood. Jeremy knew they would have to work fast to save his life.

In less than 30 minutes, the nurses prepared the operating room, and the anesthesiologist had Brian asleep. After preparing the abdomen with an antiseptic solution, Jeremy made a large incision. Jeremy removed the knife only after the abdomen was open and the full extent of the injury could be determined. The abdomen was full of blood, and active bleeding came from the depths. Jeremy pushed on the bleeding area with sponges while the nurse assistant used suction to clear the blood.

"I have no blood pressure. He has a tachycardia of 150," yelled the anesthesiologist.

"I think I have control of the bleeding now," said Jeremy calmly while applying pressure to the depths of the abdomen. "We have time, so you can pour in the intravenous fluids and get his blood pressure up before I do anything else."

After about 10 minutes of further resuscitation, the anesthesiologist got the blood pressure up to 110 / 70 and the pulse rate down to 110. "I think it is OK for you to proceed with the surgery now," said the anesthesiologist, following Jeremy's example of remaining calm.

Jeremy removed the sponge that controlled the bleeding, and blood welled up again. He clamped the aorta just below the diaphragm. He removed the sponge. No blood was flowing to the organs in the abdomen with the clamp on the aorta. Now the bleeding was manageable. The knife wound had lacerated the splenic artery. This caused most of the bleeding. There was a minor injury to the pancreas. Jeremy dissected out the splenic artery and ligated both open ends. The spleen remained viable, having a dual blood supply. Jeremy felt it was unnecessary to perform a splenectomy. He controlled the bleeding by ligating the damaged splenic artery. Jeremy removed the clamp from the aorta, and there was no further bleeding. Careful inspection of the intestines revealed miraculously that the knife damaged neither the large nor the small bowel. Satisfied there was nothing more to do, Jeremy left a drain around the pancreas and closed the abdomen. By the end of the procedure, the anesthesiologist reported that the blood pressure was now 130/80 and the pulse rate was 90. Brian was hemodynamically stable.

Chapter 42

Brian woke up in the recovery room. Jeremy's smiling face was the first thing that he saw. Brian looked around the room and saw Julie and Iona.

"It's good to have you back," Julie said excitedly.

Jeremy described the injuries and what happened during the surgery. "I think you are lucky to be alive. You lost about 2/3 of your blood volume, and we had to replace the blood with saline solution. It'll take about a month to get your blood levels back to normal."

"Thank you," said Brian. "You saved my life."

"We're even now. You saved my life the first day when you tackled the tattooed man in this hospital. That was before you even got to know if my life was worth saving!" laughed Jeremy.

Jeremy continued. "I've contacted Commander Bennett, and we still plan to go ahead with the raid on Leaf Cay in four days. Iona and Julie will stay in a safe location and manage the computer. We have some drones with infrared detection, so Julie and Iona will pass on the location of the guards to the commandos on the ground. They will also set into motion the financial destruction and transfer the money as previously arranged."

"We'll be staying at a friend's place, moving every few days to avoid another attack until this is over," said Julie. "As soon as it is medically safe, we'll move you with us so that we can take care of you. When we let you out of our sight even for a minute, look at the mess you got yourself into!" The four of them laughed, but Brian grasped his abdomen in doing so.

"Ouch," Brian whispered.

"It's time for me to prepare for the attack on Leaf Cay," said Jeremy. "I spoke with Commander Bennett, and we are almost ready. I need to move *'The Sailor'* in position. I'll lift the anchor first thing in the morning. Iona and Julie are going to stay here to look after you."

"Good luck," said Brian. "Be careful and keep in constant contact with us. We'll be your eye in the sky with our drones."

Jeremy pulled up the anchor and motored *'The Sailor'* aka *'Iona Too'* through Elizabeth Harbour to the Atlantic. The easterly trade winds made it easy to head north along the Exuma chain of islands. Jeremy steered for Staniel Cay, less than five miles from Leaf Cay. He planned to anchor the boat off Big Major Island, near Staniel Cay Yacht Club, amongst the many other sailboats. Again, he would hide in plain view. This was the best way to avoid detection. Iona and Julie would remain in Georgetown to take care of Brian. They would monitor the progress of the raid.

Jeremy enjoyed the freedom that comes with sailing by

himself. As always, when the wind filled the sails at the beginning of a trip, it overwhelmed Jeremy with happiness and contentment. The open ocean seemed to welcome him while washing away all his worries and doubts. He looked around the horizon while basking in his beautiful and happy moment. There were a few sailboats on the open ocean. Some were heading in the same north direction as he was going, but some were heading south. He wondered whether they experienced the same happy moments on their sailboats.

Hurricane season would soon be upon them, and the Bahamas was not the best location when the hurricanes came. Many parts of the Bahamas were still in disrepair from Dorian, a category five hurricane that ripped through the Bahamas four years earlier. Many people died, and there was massive destruction of houses and sailboats. Many Bahamians had little to start with, and to have that taken away by hurricanes just didn't seem fair. Many sailboats would leave the Bahamas a few weeks before the start of hurricane season in June.

Jeremy easily found a spot to anchor off Big Major Island. He lowered the dinghy and fired up the engine. He motored to Leaf Cay. Jeremy had sunglasses hiding his eyes, a large brim hat, and had covered his face to avoid recognition. He brought the image-stabilizing binoculars. Leaf Cay was a 10-minute ride. The brand-new villa looked huge. Armed guards stood on each of the three beaches and on the dock. They positioned the guards to prevent anyone from coming onto the island. There were 3 speedboats at the dock, including the red one that had intercepted him in the middle of the ocean all those months ago. Jeremy completed the circumnavigation of the island and then returned to his sailboat.

The following morning, Jeremy called Commander Bennett and met him in one of the private suites of the Staniel Cay Yacht Club. Commander Bennett sat at a small table when Jeremy walked in. He was by himself. "Are we all set for tomorrow night?" Jeremy asked.

"Yes," replied the commander. "20 of my most reliable commandos have been doing exercises at night for the past week on various islands in the Exumas. As far as they are concerned, this is just another exercise. I will inform them of the true purpose of the raid immediately before we land and that we will probably encounter some resistance. I want to ensure they do not tip us off at the last minute."

"Julie and Iona are manning the drones using the computer and will contact you as to the position of the guards. I have my Kevlar vest and will be at the back of your team as they advance so as not to get in the way. I'll bring my dinghy. After you neutralize the guards, I will have a conversation with Julian. Then you arrest him," explained Jeremy.

"For now, get plenty of rest to prepare for the long night

tomorrow," said Commander Bennett.

On returning to the boat, Jeremy stopped at the Blue Grotto. He had heard about this place and had brought his snorkeling gear. It was low tide. He tied the dinghy to a rock. He dove underneath the rock formation and entered a beautiful cavern. Multiple schools of fish swam in the cavern's shade. Sunlight beamed through an opening at the top of the cavern, giving the blue grotto a beautiful contrast of shadows and luminescence. It was truly spectacular. It confirmed to Jeremy how much of life he had left to experience. Jeremy floated on top of the water, looking at schools of fish darting from side to side and enjoying the peace of being fully immersed in nature. He imagined how every day could be like this.

The tide started coming in, bringing a strong current. Jeremy swam back to his dinghy and headed back to the sailboat. After making a sandwich for dinner, he fell asleep dreaming of the ocean. *"**The Sailor**"* rocked him gently with the small waves lapping on the hull. He woke up 12 hours later, ready to deal with whatever was going to happen.

Chapter 43

In pitch blackness, Jeremy lay flat on the beach. He arrived in his dinghy after the 20 commandos beached their boat. They disappeared into the depths of darkness on the island to surround the villa. He plugged his cell phone into his ear to be in constant communication with Julie and Iona. So far, there had been nothing to report. The drones confirmed that the guard on the beach had left, so it was a suitable spot for the commandos to gain access to Leaf Cay. Commander Bennett instructed him to stay there until he came back for him.

"Anything going on?" whispered Jeremy into his cell phone.

"Everything is quiet so far. The drone images show the guards around the villa and inside," replied Julie. "There does not appear to be anyone near you. I will wait for your instructions before I do the financial transfers."

"How's Brian?" asked Jeremy.

"He's right here beside me. Ask him yourself," said Julie.

Jeremy's phone went dead. The message on the screen said, "No signal." Jeremy thought that was strange because good cell coverage existed throughout the Bahamas. He thought about what to do next. He no longer had communication. He hoped it would not last too long, and perhaps it was just a glitch in the cell coverage. He waited. Still no signal. It had been 15 minutes. Jeremy realized something was not right. Then he heard gunfire.

Jeremy edged toward where the brush joined the beach to keep hidden. The gunfire continued. He saw the flash in the distance. He smelled the gunpowder as it drifted with the winds over the beach. Suddenly, there was rustling in the brush as the commandos came running out onto the beach. They ran towards their beached launch and began pushing it into the water. There was a lot of yelling and orders coming from several of them. They threw their guns into the launch, so they could use all their energy to push the boat from the beach. Jeremy could only count 18 out of the 20 that had come with the commander. Now they were leaving. Jeremy remained hidden. None of this made sense.

The commandos could not see Jeremy. They were almost at the water's edge, pushing their launch closer, getting ready to jump in. Commander Bennett rushed out of the brush. There was blood over his face and body. He yelled, "I will shoot anybody leaving. Get back to your posts!" Commander Bennett had his weapon drawn. He carried an M4 Carbine assault rifle capable of firing 700 rounds per minute. The commandos that were pushing the launch stopped and stared at their commander.

The self-appointed leader of the group said. "Commander Bennett, they outgunned us. If we stay, it will mean certain death.

This is a suicide mission. They were expecting us. Someone tipped them off. We will leave, so don't try to stop us."

Commander Bennett watched as they pushed the launch into the water. He knew he could not shoot them. He trained these men and met their families. His failure as a commander sank in as he watched the launch leave the beach and head into the open ocean at full throttle. He would never see these men again. They would hide on the islands and go back to the villages. The Defence Force did not have the resources to go after them, and the commandos knew that.

Jeremy watched the entire scene from where he hid. He saw Commander Bennett sit down on the beach with his hands holding his head in defeat. Jeremy approached the commander and sat down beside him. "What now?" asked Jeremy.

"They are right," said the commander, wiping the blood from his mouth. "This is a suicide mission. Two of my commandos tipped off our attack to the guards. This type of deception is common. The lure of making a lot of money is irresistible for many of my highly trained commandos. The annual salary of our commandos is about $18,000 a year. Typically, these drug operators pay their guards about $100,000 a year. They often get a bonus for signing up.

The only ones left are you and me. They have at least 20

guards, plus two of my commandos. Someone positioned them strategically to fend off an attack. If the two of us tried to storm the villa, we would get picked off and killed after only two feet from the attack."

Jeremy tried to assimilate what had just happened. After all this planning and then being defeated was too much for him to bear. "What the fuck do we do now?" Jeremy asked.

"Let me think for a moment." Said the commander.

They both sat in silence on the beach. It was approaching midnight under a moonless night. There was a gentle breeze from the east. It was warm and quiet. The small waves lap on the sand. Julian outmaneuvered Jeremy once again. This pattern repeated. Jeremy had been unsuccessful in reversing this. Perhaps knowledge was the one thing they had over Julian. They knew of his identity; they had his banking information, and now they had details of his operation on Leaf Cay.

"I have failed as a commander. I am unable to apprehend the criminals on this island. But most of all, I have failed you, Jeremy," said Commander Bennett. "Part of me wants to storm the villa. I would take many of those criminals before they blow me away. Part of me wants to protect you because I know you would probably follow me if I did that."

It took exactly 3 seconds. Commander Bennett pulled out his

pistol and placed the barrel in his mouth. He pulled the trigger. The force of the blast caused the commander to fall on his back. Brain tissue leaked through the hole in the back of his skull. He remained motionless.

"Noooo!" screamed Jeremy. "No. No." was all he could say. Jeremy hung his head as his eyes teared up. Commander Bennett was perhaps the only honest Defence Force officer left in the Bahamas, and now he was gone.

Behind him, Jeremy could hear the footsteps of the guards running toward him to investigate the source of the gunshot. Jeremy leaped to his feet and sprinted across the sand to his beached dinghy. He pulled it into the water and fired up the engine. Using the full throttle, he headed out into the Atlantic Ocean, circled around Staniel Cay, and then back to his sailboat. He pulled up the anchor of ***"The Sailor"*** and headed back to Georgetown to grieve. He knew that this would be a tough time for Brian and Julie.

Chapter 44

The retirement party was a lavish affair. They held the event at The Four Seasons Hotel on Yorkville Street in downtown Toronto. Society magazine reporters joined the mayor at the event. The senior executives from the hospital, along with many board members from the hospital, were there to honor Dr. Robert Planter. The chief of psychiatry made the sudden decision to retire. He stated it was for personal reasons, along with his desire to spend more time with his family. He told the hospital board that he achieved as much as possible during his tenure as chief of the Department of Psychiatry. It was time for someone else to take that rein of leadership and bring his department of psychiatry to the next level.

The dinner was exquisite, with a 7-course meal. The servers wore black tuxedos with white ties. There were over 200 guests. The hospital generated a video of doctors and nurses that Robert had worked with over the last few years. The video showed them honoring him while describing how much they would miss him. They included testimonials from some grateful patients about how he was a brilliant doctor with accolades. They wanted him to have a wonderful retirement full of happiness and splendor.

The hospital's CEO gave a touching speech outlining his achievements and how Robert was leaving the hospital a better place. He discussed his successes at fundraising and how the research was such a big part of the Department of Psychiatry, thanks to Dr. Robert Planter. He presented him with an achievement award and informed the audience about a named conference room after him.

There were a lot of congratulatory backslapping and kind words about the great things Robert had done. Overall, it was a night to remember for many who had attended. It had been a glamorous affair, with many flutes of champagne consumed along with expensive Courvoisier Brandy. The cuisine was outstanding. At midnight, the last of the guests departed.

Robert Planter flew to Nassau early the next day and caught a connecting flight to Staniel Cay. He was now sitting in the living room in the villa of Leaf Cay with his new friend Andy Smith. "Julian, it will take me a long time to get used to calling you Andy," he laughed.

"I think we are in for a great ride," said Julian. "Except for the problems we've had with Jeremy, I would have to say we had a successful transition. I think that the chapter involving Jeremy has ended. Nothing is stopping us from success, fame, and fortune."

"I'll be organizing the distribution network for our product. I plan to begin my new identity once John Papadopoulos has everything in place," said Robert. "The Bahamas seems to be the best place to buy an island and have protection. The 10% of profits flowing to my Panamanian accounts should be more than enough to keep me safe."

"We will soon have the biggest operation in the world. Our mixture of remifentanil/cocaine will be in such enormous demand that we will have trouble keeping up with the production," said Julian.

Robert smiled. This is what he had been waiting for all his life. Financial success. Julian knew how to do this right, and Robert was confident that he had made the right decision with the move to the Bahamas. He appreciated his good fortune. Life on the islands and living the dream of excesses and decadence. This was going to be easy. He felt invincible. He smiled again at the way things were turning out.

Chapter 45

The funeral for Commander Bennett was in a small church at the top of a hill in Georgetown. A few close friends and others from his village attended the service. The minister gave a touching eulogy about his kindness and commitment to his country and fellow Bahamians. Julie and Brian both had something to say, describing him as a rare human who was far too good a person for this world and how he may be in a better place now. His brother, Herman, gave a great eulogy describing how he tried to follow his example.

At the back of the church, sitting in the last pew by himself, was a bald man with a beard and sunglasses. Jeremy slid next to him. "Julian, I know why you are here."

Julian looked up at him and smiled. "I had nothing to do with the commander's death. You were there. He killed himself."

Jeremy said, "You are here to gloat. Do you think that you have neutralized me? I have been wanting to have this conversation with you. You have finished with your life as you know it. Your financial empire is about to be destroyed, and we will reveal your identity to the world. When that happens, I want you to know I am responsible for that."

Julian stared at Jeremy as he slid out of the pew and back to his friends and wife at the front of the church.

"We make our move tonight," Jeremy whispered to Brian and Julie.

It was dark. Brian and Jeremy hunched over the computer. Brian was 2 weeks out of his surgery, and the healing resulted in much less discomfort. Jeremy removed the skin stitches and the drain a week ago. The wound healed beautifully. Brian remained a little weak, but his blood levels had risen rapidly with the iron infusions. He lost a few pounds, but he convinced himself that might be good. He slept well now and was eager to be part of the team that would bring down Julian and his drug empire.

They had gone over this plan many times and had many practice runs. A direct attack on the island could not defeat Julian. Julian had increased the security forces even further. There were at least 40 men on the property now. Brian and Jeremy flew the drones over the island at high altitudes. The cameras had excellent resolution. The drones were invisible from the ground. They knew where to find the hidden cocaine, the exact location of their production facility, and how to disable the entire operation. They successfully conscripted Herman, Commander Bennett's younger brother, to help.

Herman was devastated by his brother's death. He always admired his older brother. Herman earned a degree in chemical engineering from Carleton University in Ottawa. He moved back to the Bahamas 10 years ago. His area of interest was explosives. They employed him as a senior manager in the Bahamian government. During the weekends and evenings, he scoured the internet on explosive-related websites and chat rooms. Herman was upset that his brother had not come to him for advice. The days of attacking with ground forces are long gone. Using drones with explosives was the way to go. This avoids unnecessary deaths and is a lot more accurate.

Herman approached Brian with his skills. Using a drone with a grenade was the simplest way to destroy a target on the ground. A grenade will explode 6 seconds after the drone removes the pin and descends 176 meters. A drone can hover over the top of a target and calculate the distance before dropping the grenade. The drones are so small they can escape detection from even the most sophisticated equipment. Brian and Jeremy planned to use this to destroy Julian's facility. They practiced using this on the open ocean when nobody was around. They determined that the optimal distance above the ground to release the grenade was 120 meters. This allowed an extra second so that the maximum damage occurred when the grenade exploded.

Commander Bennett left Brian and Jeremy with an arsenal full of grenades and other weapons. They each had two types of drones that they would fly. One drone would stay at around 3000 feet and send back constant information; the other smaller drones would get within 120 meters of the targets. It was a clear night with little wind, perfect for the drone attack.

Julie and Iona were sitting at a separate computer. Working with Derek, they perfected how to disrupt the financial empire and transfer the money to the various governments' coffers as taxes. They hoped there would be major chaos to allow the time necessary for the transfer. The plan to deplete all accounts of Julian required about 15 minutes of confusion to ensure the process was irreversible. After that time, there was no way they could transfer the money back because of the firewalls that Derek had created. When Brian and Jeremy destroyed the island's production facility, Derek, Iona, and Julie began the transfer process. This entire process would take a few hours. Once started, it could not be reversed. The stir created by the drone attack would prevent detection of the money transfer until the process was past the point of no return.

Jeremy and Brian located where they stored the cocaine underground. Before his murder, Jose sent the plans via email. A series of tunnels connected the facility to mix the cocaine with the remifentanil. They automated the entire process so there would be few workers involved to protect the product's integrity. This would reduce the chance of employee theft. They packaged the final product into single-dose containers. Plastic boxes held 100 single dose packages and stored them in rows of 50 high and 50 deep. Their goal was to eradicate this production line.

Six air vents came out of the ground strategically to ensure good air circulation in the tunnel system. This prevented too much heat from developing and reduced the possibility of fires. Carefully placed shrubs hid these air vents. Each air vent was 6 inches wide. Jeremy and Brian locked their precise GPS coordinates into the drones. There were six of them, and the accuracy of the grenades was such that the air vents were certain to be hit. The weight of the grenade would destroy the plastic screen, which covered the air vents on impact. The extra second would allow the grenades to fall into the underground tunnels so that they would create the maximum damage. They had six drones that would simultaneously hit each of the six air vents.

They programmed the drones to release the grenades at precisely one minute past midnight. This would cause chaos and unrest, allowing the team to begin the complicated electronic financial destruction.

"Let's do another dry run," said Brian. The drone at 3000 feet gave them accurate video images, even through the darkness. They saw the guards walk on the beach and around the villa's perimeter. They brought the smaller drones down to their position 120 meters above the air vents they would bomb. On individual screens, they could see the air vent targets and determined that they accurately fixed the grenades to land in their GPS position.

"That looks pretty good," said Jeremy. "It looks like they are in an excellent position when we release the grenades."

"Perfect," said Brian. "Let's pull them back up to 2000 feet, out of the way until closer to midnight."

Julie and Iona sat in front of a computer next to them. "We are ready to activate as soon as we confirm the attack was successful. Make as much chaos for us as possible!" said Iona.

Chapter 46

Julian, John, and Robert sat on the balcony overlooking the private marina. 3 powerboats bobbed gently in the water. They were smoking cigars and sipping cognac. John Papadopoulos flew in that morning. He brought all the information about Robert's new identity. This included visa cards, driver's licenses, passports, and social insurance numbers. He would be Frederick Burnstein, an expatriated Canadian originally from Ottawa. Frederick was five years younger than Robert but had lived in the Bahamas for the last five years. Frederick Burnstein failed to return from a scuba diving trip a few months ago.

"It's been a great day," said Robert. "I set the distribution network up so that there is no way anyone can trace it back to us on Leaf Cay. Authorities confiscate less than 10% of the drugs entering the United States. The way we have set things up, it is likely that less than 1% of our product will get confiscated. We will still use the Metropolitan Hospital in Toronto as a major hub, and that process is almost 100% automated. No one even knows that we are using them. From that hub, we will re-establish the distribution we had established before. We will supply the major urban centers in the United States."

"I expect to double our revenue within three years up to $6 billion," said Julian. "Things have never looked better."

The three of them felt the ground shake at the same time. It started as a mild tremor but intensified to where the shaking marble floor cracked with the movement. The villa's walls moved, and a loud creaking noise roared from within the depths of the villa. It knocked the ashes off their cigars, and their cognac spilled. "What the hell?" cried out Julian. They raced down the spiral staircase and out the front door.

There appeared streams of fire coming out of the ground at several places around them, lighting up the sky. The streams of fire extended 30 feet. Fine gray dust covering everything rained down on them. At first, they were not sure what was going on. Julian thought maybe there was an earthquake or some underground disturbance that set things off.

One guard ran to them and said, "Boss, there's been an explosion. We must get you out of here."

"What are you talking about?" screamed Julian. "How's that possible?"

"Don't know right now, boss," said the guard. "Let's get you down to the beach house to be safe."

The guard hustled them down to the beach house and closed the door behind them. Julian fired up the computer to look at the security system. He saw videos of the lines of fire coming from at least six areas. "The fire seems to come from the air vents," said

Julian. "There must have been an internal combustion explosion in the tunnels. The engineers said that would not be possible because of the great circulation system afforded by the air vent system. It doesn't make any sense."

Suddenly, there was an e-mail alert that came up. Julian clicked on the alert. "There is some unusual activity in your bank account. Click on this link for more information." Just as Julian clicked on the link, another alert came up, then another, then another. Before he understood what had happened, there were over 100 alerts on his computer screen. More alerts were coming, all saying the same thing. He placed an urgent call to his banker in Panama. His personal cell phone number was on his contact list, but there was no answer. It was one in the morning.

Julian kept staring at the screen. Finally, the alerts stopped coming in. He clicked into his bank account and logged in with his password that only he knew, or so he thought. The largest bank account had over $3 billion, was now empty. He logged into the next ten bank accounts with accounts over $100 million, but they were also empty.

Robert stared at the screen. "Is this a cyber-attack?" He asked.

Julian stared at the computer screen and said one word. *"Jeremy."*

When the first light came, John, Robert and Julian toured to look at the extent of the damage to the island. The villa had major cracks in many of the walls. Large chunks of plaster covered the marble floors in all the rooms. All the marble floors had cracked, and some cracks were about 6 inches wide. The chandeliers and lights hung by electrical cords, swinging slightly in the breeze. In the kitchen, pots and pans covered the floor. Broken china and glass spread out everywhere. The electricity had disconnected. The only light in the building came through the skylights and the broken windows.

They descended into the tunnel that attached to the basement of the house. Nothing remained of the cocaine or remifentanil. It vaporized into a fine gray powder. There was destruction everywhere, with parts of the tunnel collapsed. There was nothing left of the automated system to mix and package the drugs. Everything was gone.

John Papadopoulos looked down at the stump of the little finger of his right hand. The scar healed nicely and was barely noticeable. It astonished John that no one noticed he was missing a finger. He had not talked about what happened with anybody, including Julian. He knew Jeremy was behind this plant's destruction, but he also somehow hacked into Julian's bank accounts. This would be a major problem because many drug dealers had already paid for their shipments. Such is the drug business, upfront payment before any delivery. Now there was no shipment, and there was no money to refund them.

John's finances were totally separate from this drug operation. Knowing a thing or two about illegal activities, John was not prepared to take the risk down the path of drug production. He witnessed too many of his business associates come to an untimely death. Others simply disappeared. His role was to transfer the new identity to Robert Planter and collect his generous fee. It was his bad luck that the attack on the island occurred during this visit. Looking to take advantage of any situation, he pondered his options. John's only concern about what happened to Julian was to turn this to his advantage.

Julian raged. He did 3 lines of cocaine, trying to calm his rattled nerves. The drug only made him agitated. "I need to know how that little prick did this. The drug operation we can rebuild, but I need to get that money back. Otherwise, we are all fucked."

Robert said, "Let's drag him here and then beat it out of him. We won't stop until we get our money back."

"Exactly how are you going to do that?" asked Julian.

"I have a plan," said John, taking control now that he had time to think.

Chapter 47

Jeremy was totally exhausted when he fell into bed that night. He stayed up for over 24 hours, planning the attack on Leak Cay with Brian. The drone images of the fire coming out of the air vents were spectacular. The destruction was far more extensive than they expected. They witnessed three men running out of the house. Jeremy and Brian saw these three men stare at the fire from the ground. They watched the guard accompany them to the beach house. At 4:00 AM, the fire settled down, and all was quiet on the island. At first light, they witnessed the same three men look at the destruction and then disappear into what is left of the villa.

Iona and Julie confirmed they had indeed emptied the bank accounts. They successfully transferred the money to the tax departments in Canada and the Bahamas. Some tax advisers in these two countries would scratch their heads trying to understand from where the money came. The financial destruction of Julian occurred without a hitch.

Both Brian and Jeremy sensed relief that they had accomplished this formidable task. The destruction of a drug empire and the evil men behind this facility satisfied the goal of making the Bahamas a better place. They had done a good deed for society and for themselves. Julian would have attempted to destroy both of them had they failed. By the time they went to bed, the anxiety they had experienced over the past few days had disappeared. When Brian and Jeremy fell asleep, their dreams were full of pleasant visions of a certain future.

In the dark Bahamian night, men dressed in black crawled quietly over the finely trimmed lawn of the house in February Point. They had blacked out their faces with paint. They wore black one-piece workout attire. No one could see them. They wore gas masks and breathed in the air from a canister. They knew four of them were in the house, but they were only going to take Jeremy. There were six of them in case they ran across some resistance. The security alarm in the house posed no concern for them. They planned to be long gone by the time it activated.

One man approached the intake vent for fresh air circulation into the house. He opened a gas canister and released the vaporized contents into the vent. After waiting 10 minutes, he released another canister of gas. Another 10 minutes passed before they entered the house. The beeping of the alarm started. The alarm would sound in one minute, giving them a narrow window to act. They exited the house within 30 seconds, carrying an unconscious Jeremy slung over one of their backs. They hopped onto the speedboat that waited at the pier and sprinted into the Atlantic Ocean. Within an hour, they docked the boat at Leaf Cay.

Jeremy woke up confused. With his hands and legs bound,

he sat in a chair. He did not recognize the room. He noticed the plaster on the walls had cracked, and the marble floor had cracked too. The only natural light came in through the skylights and the windows. He tried to raise himself from the chair, but it firmly attached the zip ties to his arms and legs to the wooden chair. The tightness of the ties prevented any movement. His throat was dry, and he felt nauseated.

Julian, Robert, and John entered the room and sat in a row of chairs before him. "Did you really think you could get away from us?" asked Julian. He was pointing a gun at Jeremy.

Jeremy stared at him. Julian's bloodshot eyes darted around the room. He fixed his attention on Jeremy. The dilated pupils shone like beacons boring into Jeremy. The rhythmic movement of his knee bounced up and down in a frantic, spastic motion.

"I want my money back," said Julian.

"That will not be possible," said Jeremy. "We employed a banking IT expert to install firewalls to prevent any reverse transaction. All that money went to the tax departments of the Bahamas and Canada. There's no way to retrieve it."

"I don't believe you," said Julian.

"It doesn't really matter what you believe," said Jeremy. "We financially ruined you. We destroyed your drug operation here.

As of later today, Andy Smith will be the most wanted man in the world. Your name is going viral on social media and every newscast. There is nowhere for you to hide."

Julian passed the gun to John. "John, shoot him. This was your idea to bring him here, and it is a total waste of time."

John took the gun and aimed it at Jeremy. Jeremy closed his eyes. This was the ending he feared. He thought of Iona. At least they spared her. He worried that his death would cause unspeakable pain for her. They truly lived together as soulmates. Because of the terrible ordeals over the past few months, they became closer. The idea of inflicting sadness and suffering on her devastated him. He heard a loud gunshot; then he heard another one. He opened his eyes. Julian and Robert were lying on the floor with blood and liquified brain tissue oozing out of the holes in their foreheads.

"They were pretty much dead, anyway. There was no way the drug distributors would let them get away with losing all their money. I did Julian and Robert a favor. They knew too much about me and my business. I do not want to be looking over my shoulder for the rest of my life," said John.

Jeremy was stunned. After what he had done to John by cutting off his finger and the associated humiliation, John had not used this opportunity to put a bullet into his head. "Why don't you just pull the trigger on me now and get it over?" asked Jeremy.

John said, "Jeremy, I admire your principles and fearlessness. I don't believe that you are any danger to me. You were right to go after Julian; otherwise, he would have eventually destroyed you. Me, you will never see me again. I am the master of identity theft, and I will disappear. I see no need to complicate my life by putting a bullet into your brain. Someone as clever as Iona would not stop chasing me. That would not be worth it for me. I always like to use my advantage to improve my lot in life. Besides, if you ever encounter me again, you will not recognize me."

With that, John got up, dropped the gun on the floor, and left the room. Jeremy heard the thunder of the speedboat as the engines revved. He heard the engine droning disappear as the boat traveled further from the island. Soon, all he heard was the gentle breeze as it blew through the open walls of the house and the quiet surf as it washed on the beach.

Chapter 48

Jeremy and Iona found themselves in Luperon, Dominican Republic. Late June arrived, along with the start of hurricane season. Most of the hurricanes came in September and October. Their plan was to head south to Granada out of the hurricane belt. They met many sailors in Luperon who had similar plans over the past few days. Some waited for a good weather window before heading south. Some still waited 3 years after they first arrived in the Dominican Republic. They appeared to be afraid to make the move south. Sailing to Granada from the Dominican Republic was difficult because the trade winds came from the east. An 800-mile journey battling against the wind and through rough seas for 7 days was not something that most sailors were willing to suffer.

Jeremy and Iona were content to wait for a change in the winds. They were in no rush to go anywhere. They lived day to day. If the urge to head back to Toronto seized them, their plan was to wait until that urge passed and stay put. They were happy to spend time with each other without the drama of the past few months. Their plan involved waiting to see which way the wind blew and then heading in that direction. They heard there may be a weather window for heading south on Wednesday, but perhaps it might be the week after. Either way, it was fine with them. They had everything they needed with each other on *Iona Too*.

The End

About the Author

John Hagen is a retired surgeon from the Toronto area. He spends the summers sailing on Lake Ontario. He spent the past 2 winter seasons cruising his 51-foot sailboat in the Bahamas and the Caribbean. He writes about his adventures on his sailing blog www.dreamingofileana.com